KB067489

나의 클린트 이스트우드

〈K-픽션〉 시리즈는 한국문학의 젊은 상상력입니다. 최근 발표된 가장 우수하고 흥미로운 작품을 엄선하여 출간하는 〈K-픽션〉은 한국문학의 생생한 현장을 국내외 독자들과 실시간으로 공유하고자 기획되었습니다. 〈바이링궐 에디션 한국 대표 소설〉 시리즈를 통해 검증된 탁월한 번역진이 참여하여 원작의 재미와 품격을 최대한 살린 〈K-픽션〉 시리즈는 매 계절마다 새로운 작품을 선보입니다.

This 〈K-Fiction〉 Series represents the brightest of young imaginative voices in contemporary Korean fiction. Each issue consists of a wide range of outstanding contemporary Korean short stories that the editorial board of ***Asia*** carefully selects each season. These stories are then translated by professional Korean literature translators, all of whom take special care to faithfully convey the pieces' original tones and grace. We hope that, each and every season, these exceptional young Korean voices will delight and challenge all of you, our treasured readers both here and abroad.

K-Fiction Series

나의 클린트 이스트우드
My Clint Eastwood

오한기 | 전승희 옮김
Written by Oh Han-ki
Translated by Jeon Seung-hee

ASIA
PUBLISHERS

Contents

나의 클린트 이스트우드
My Clint Eastwood

클린트 이스트우드. 그는 잘빠진 서부의 영웅이었고 행동 하나하나에 멋이 밴 강력계 형사였다. 아카데미를 휩쓴 영화감독이었으며 모범적인 공화당원이기도 했다. 1986년에는 캘리포니아 주 카멜 시 시장으로 당선되기도 했다. 그는 부정부패를 척결한 뒤 미련 없이 시장직에서 물러났다. 그는 여러모로 완벽한 남자였다.

영화에서 드러나는 클린트 이스트우드의 세계관은 고전적이다. 그가 만든 영화뿐만 아니라 젊은 시절의 그가 출연한 영화를 보면 누구나 그 사실을 알 수 있다. 〈황야의 무법자〉에서 그는 권총 한 자루를 들고 특유의 무정부주의적인 태도로 약자를 위해 타락한 공권력과

Clint Eastwood was a dashing Westerns hero, a rogue police officer in charge of violent crimes, a figure whose every gesture and movement seemed to embody cool. He is an Oscar-winning film director and a model Republican. He was elected mayor of Carmel-by-the-Sea. He cleaned up much of the corruption in city hall but did not seek re-election. He was a perfect man in many ways.

Clint Eastwood embodies a classical worldview in his films. This fact is clear not only in the movies he's directed, but also in those he's starred in. In *A Fistful of Dollars*, he fights against corrupt authorities with nothing but a single pistol. In a characteristically anarchistic manner—he fights for the sake

싸우고 악인을 처단한다. 자신이 믿는 가치를 절대적으로 숭배하는 것이다. 감동은 여기에서 온다.

자그마한 영화잡지에서 기자 일을 하고 있을 때, 나는 클린트 이스트우드가 공화당원이라는 이유로 그의 영화를 폄하하는 동료를 본 적이 있었다. 동료는 알랭 레네와 장 뤽 고다르의 영화를 찬양하며 클린트 이스트우드를 비판했다. 혁명적이고 진보적인 《카이에 뒤 시네마》의 일원들과 비교해 클린트 이스트우드가 폭력적이고 단순하다는 것이었다. 별다른 반론을 내세우진 않았지만 내 생각은 달랐다. 알랭 레네와 장 뤽 고다르의 영화가 현란하고 난해한 건 나약하기 짝이 없는 자아에 대한 반작용이었다. 나는 동료와 다시는 클린트 이스트우드에 대해 이야기하지 않았다.

클린트 이스트우드는 이제 늙었다. 그가 감독이기 이전에 배우였다는 사실을 아는 이는 드물다. 특히 젊은 여자들은 그의 쇠약한 육체와 과거의 강인함을 함께 떠올리지 못한다. 그저 깐깐해 보이는 노감독 정도로 기억할 뿐이다. 어쩌면 호르몬의 문제일지도 모른다. 중년이 지나 목소리와 머리칼이 얇아지고 있는 남자들…… 알랭 들롱, 미키 루크, 알 파치노, 로버트 드 니

of the disempowered and punishes villains. He is absolutely faithful to the values he believes in. This is why he moves us.

When I was working as a reporter for a small movie magazine, a colleague despised Clint Eastwood just because he was a Republican. He praised Alain Resnais and Jean Luc Goddard while discounting the films of Clint Eastwood. He argued that Clint Eastwood was violent and simplistic in comparison to the progressive and revolutionary members of the Cahiers du cinéma. Although I didn't refute his argument, I had a different opinion. To me, it seemed that Alain Resnais and Jean Luc Goddard made their films dazzlingly obscure only to compensate for their pathetic personalities. I never discussed Clint Eastwood again with him.

Clint Eastwood is old now. These days, people rarely know that he was once an actor before he was a director. Young women, especially, don't have memories of his tough guy past behind his now frail old body. They know him only as an old, hard-grained director. The change in his appearance is probably a matter of hormones. Men lose their voice and hair after they become middle-aged. Alain Delon, Micky Rourke, Al Pacino, Robert De Niro... All they can do these days is to take on

로…… 지금 그들이 할 수 있는 거라곤 쇠락한 옛 명성을 보전하기 위해 시시껄렁한 조연을 맡아 고군분투하는 것뿐이다. 〈옛날 옛적 서부에서〉의 찰스 브론슨처럼 하모니카만 갖고도 내면의 멋을 풍기는 남자는 이제 찾을 수 없다. 우리는 예산이 부족해 냉난방도 제대로 되지 않는 시네마테크를 제외하고는 진정한 남자들을 볼 수 없다.

반면 우디 앨런은 늙어서도 인기를 끌고 있다. 전형적인 뉴요커인 우디 앨런은 쉴 틈 없이 연애를 하고 입을 놀린다. 우디 앨런을 추종하는 이들은 그가 영화에 대단한 철학이라도 불어넣은 것처럼 말한다. 클린트 이스트우드가 총알 하나로 우디 앨런의 수다보다 많은 것을 말하고 있다는 사실도 모르고 말이다. 우디 앨런이 연인에게 우리가 헤어지는 이유에 대해 집요하게 설명하는 동안, 클린트 이스트우드는 하룻밤을 함께 보낸 여자를 총으로 쏜 뒤 뒤도 안 돌아보고 모텔 방을 벗어나 포드의 시동을 걸 수 있지 않을까? 언젠가 우디 앨런을 찬양해 마지않는 여자에게 〈애니 홀〉을 좋아한다고 한 적이 있지만 사실은 아니다. 클린트 이스트우드처럼 항상 총을 지니고 있는 것까지는 아니더라도 가끔씩은

trivial supporting roles and work to live up to their withering legacy. It's impossible now to find an old man who has the sort of inner zest that Charles Bronson showed with a single harmonica in hand in *Once Upon a Time in the West*. These days we can't find any true men other than in the Cinématèque archives, which aren't even temperature-controlled due to budget problems.

On the other hand, Woody Allen is still popular even though he's old. A typical New Yorker, Woody Allen continues to have love affairs and chatter on and on. Woody Allen fans dare to claim that he's imbued the genre of movie with some sort of great philosophy. They don't know that Clint Eastwood says a lot more with a single bullet than Woody Allen does with all his talk. While Woody Allen keeps on explaining to his lovers why they have to go their own separate ways, Clint Eastwood would most likely just shoot the woman he just spent the night with and leave his motel room to start the engine of his Ford. I once told a woman who worshiped Woody Allen that I liked *Annie Hall*. But that was a lie. We may not need to always carry a gun around like Clint Eastwood in order to make our way through this hard life, but we can't avoid lying from time to time.

거짓말을 해야 이 고단한 현실을 헤쳐나갈 수 있는 법이다.

따지자면 나는 클린트 이스트우드보다 우디 앨런에 가까웠다. 몸은 빼빼 말랐고 눈은 지독히 나빴으며 할 줄 아는 건 수다뿐이었다. 잡지사를 그만둔 뒤 더 그렇게 됐다. 우디 앨런과 다른 점이 있다면 여자에게 인기가 없다는 것뿐이었다. 아무도 이런 내가 클린트 이스트우드와 한때 가까운 사이였다는 사실을 믿지 않을 것이다.

클린트 이스트우드를 만난 건 지난해 가을이었다. 나는 당시 위암에 걸린 숙부를 대신해 펜션과 낚시터를 관리하고 있었다. 자녀가 없었던 숙부는 나를 펜션에 남기고 요양원으로 떠났다. 묘지가 가득한 뒷산과 근처 도살장에서 흘러내려온 오수로 오염된 저수지…… 토지개발마저 내팽개쳐버린 〈OK목장의 결투〉의 닷지 시티 같은 펜션에 대체 누가 묵는단 말인가. 손님이 하도 없어서 전염병 환자라도 관리할 수 있을 정도였다. 마땅히 할 일이 없었던 나는 작가들이 고독을 양분 삼아 걸작을 써낸 것을 떠올렸고 시나리오를 쓰기 시작했다. 그러나 성과는 없었다. 내 생각엔 흠잡을 데 없는 대본

Actually, the fact is I'm a lot more like Woody Allen than Clint Eastwood. I'm skinny, my eyesight is extremely poor, and I'm only good at talking. This was even truer after I quit my job at the magazine company. The only difference between Woody Allen and me is that I'm not as popular with the ladies. So nobody would believe me if I said I was once close with Clint Eastwood.

I met Clint Eastwood last fall. At that time I was managing a guesthouse and a fishing spot for my uncle who had been diagnosed with stomach cancer. As my uncle didn't have his own children, he entrusted me with the house and the spot and left for a nursing home. There was a hill full of graves behind the guesthouse, and the reservoir in front was polluted with dirty water from a nearby slaughterhouse. Who would stay in that guesthouse? I wondered. It was like Dodge City in *Gunfire at the O.K. Corral,* a place abandoned even by land developers. Guests were so rare that I could have run a facility there for quarantined patients. As I had nothing else to do, I began to write film scenarios. I remembered that writers nurtured in solitude produced masterpieces. But my writing ventures were not successful. Although I thought my scenarios were flawless, they failed again and again

이었지만 공모전에서는 연달아 떨어졌으니 말이다. 그러니 영화를 보고 시간을 축내며 언제 올지 모르는 손님이나 기다리는 수밖에.

주로 오는 손님은 낚시꾼이다. 그들은 대개 혼자였으며 말수가 적고 낯을 가렸다. 매달 두어 명 정도 이곳에 왔는데 선입견인지는 몰라도 나는 그들이 왠지 께름칙했다. 낚시꾼들은 대부분 조용히 왔다 떠났지만 가끔 말썽을 일으켰다. 지난여름 낚시꾼들 중 하나가 저수지에 빠졌다. 깊은 저수지는 그를 숨겼고 나는 신고하지 않았다. 안개가 자욱한 날은 새벽낚시가 금지였는데도 그는 내 경고를 무시했던 것이었다. 몇 가지 사건이 더 있었지만 낚시꾼을 입에 담지 않는 건 펜션을 관리하면서 생긴 불문율이다.

가끔은 특별한 목적이 있는 사람들도 왔다. 손님이 부른 창녀를 제외하면 몸을 숨기고 싶어 하는 사람들이 대부분이었다. 빚에 쫓기거나. 사람에 쫓기거나. 둘 중 하나였다. 그중 하나가 클린트 이스트우드였다.

클린트 이스트우드가 처음 관리실에 들어왔을 때 나는 그가 한국전쟁에 관한 영화를 찍기 위해 답사를 왔거나, 부인 몰래 한국인 유학생과 밀애를 즐기다 이곳

when I submitted them to competitions. So I had no choice but to waste my time watching movies and waiting for guests that just might show up.

Most guests were anglers. They came alone, and were quiet, and didn't want to hang out with other people. There were several guests per month. I might be prejudiced, but I never felt comfortable around them. Most of them came and went quietly, but occasionally there were those who caused trouble. An angler drowned last summer. The deep reservoir hid his body, and I never reported it to the police. Although I warned him that angling was forbidden at dawn on a foggy day, he ignored my warning. There were a few more incidents, but it was an unwritten rule I learned while managing the guesthouse not to report anything that happened to the anglers.

Occasionally, people with specific purposes came. Except for the hookers that some guests invited, most of these people were in hiding. They were either being chased by their debts or by other people. One of these guests happened to be Clint Eastwood.

When he first showed up at my office, I thought he might have come for a site visit for his movie about the Korean War. Or, he could have been fol-

까지 따라왔을 거라고 생각했다. 선글라스로 얼굴을 가렸지만 나는 단번에 그가 클린트 이스트우드라는 것을 알아챘다. 수많은 여자들을 유혹한 그를 어찌 못 알아볼 수 있겠나.

"방 있나?"

그가 특유의 가래 끓는 목소리로 물었다. 그리고 내가 자신을 알아본 것을 이미 알고 있다는 듯 희미하게 웃었다.

"돈만 있다면요."

내가 답했다. 솔직히 말해 나는 그에게 실망했다. 그는 영화에서 봤던 것보다 볼품없었다. 노년의 멋을 풍기는 것도 아니었고 허리는 구부정했으며 온몸에 주름이 가득했으니 말이다.

클린트 이스트우드가 펜션에 묵은 지 열흘이 지나서였다. 나는 그에 대한 기사들을 검색해봤다. 지난여름 미국 언론들은 일제히 클린트 이스트우드가 제작자와 다툼 끝에 행방불명됐다고 보도했다. 할리우드 작업환경의 급격한 변화와 분업 체계에 적응하지 못한 클린트 이스트우드가 제작자에게 상해를 입히고 계약금을 빼

lowing his secret lover here, a Korean student abroad. Although he hid his eyes behind his sunglasses, I immediately recognized him. How could you not recognize the man who had seduced so many women?

"Do you have a room?" he asked in his characteristic raspy voice. Then he smiled vaguely as if acknowledging that he knew that I recognized him.

"If you can pay for it," I answered. Frankly, I was disappointed. He looked much less attractive in real life than he did in movies. He didn't look cool as an old man. He was slightly bent and his face was full of wrinkles.

For the first ten days Clint Eastwood stayed in the guesthouse, I searched through news articles about him. All the newspapers reported that the previous summer Clint Eastwood had run away after a quarrel with his producer. Having failed to adjust to rapid changes and the new division of labor system in the Hollywood work environment, it was reported that he had injured his producer and run away somewhere overseas, taking the down payment for the movie with him. Some media outlets speculated that he was most likely hiding in Cuba or Mexico. They had no clue whatsoever that he was actually

돌려 외국으로 도주했다는 내용이었다. 언론들은 유력한 은신처로 쿠바와 멕시코를 꼽았는데, 그가 한국에 있다는 걸 짐작조차 못하는 모양이었다. 기사에 따르면 클린트 이스트우드는 신작에 대해 토론을 하던 중 의견 차가 생기자 급기야 제작자에게 총까지 겨누었다고 한다. 그 제작자는 지난 20년 동안 클린트 이스트우드가 꾸준히 영화를 만들 수 있도록 지원해 준 건실한 사업가였다. 클린트 이스트우드의 영화가 매번 적자를 내는데도 노감독에 대한 예우 차원에서 말이다.

"당신이 뭘 알아?"

클린트 이스트우드는 제작자에게 총을 겨누며 이렇게 말했다고 한다. 그러나 언론들은 진짜 아무것도 모르는 건 클린트 이스트우드라고 보도했다. 그는 더 이상 서부의 영웅이 아니었다. 아무런 명분도 없이 폭력을 행사하고 푼돈을 빼돌린 추잡한 도망자일 뿐이었다. 내가 판단하기에도 클린트 이스트우드는 자격지심에 기회를 놓친 고집 센 늙은이에 불과했다. 나는 이 사실이 전 세계로 보도되고 있다는 것을 그에게 말하지 않았다. 자신이 망신을 당하고 있다는 것을 알면 〈알카트라스 탈출〉의 탈옥수 모리스처럼 무슨 일을 저지를지

in Korea. According to these articles, Clint Eastwood had aimed a gun at his producer when their discussion on their new movie had become contentious. That producer was a solid businessman who had supported Clint Eastwood through his filmmaking for the past two decades. He continued to support Clint Eastwood to pay his respects to the old director, although his movies had always gone into the red.

It was reported that Clint Eastwood had aimed his gun at his producer and asked, "What the hell do you know?" According to the same articles, however, it was Clint Eastwood who hadn't known a thing. He was no longer the Western hero. He was a reviled fugitive who had become violent for no justifiable reason and had stolen a petty sum of money. It seemed even to me that he was a stubborn old man who had lost his chance to make another film because of his pathetic pride. I didn't tell him, though, that what he had done was being reported all across the world. If he knew that his name was being disgraced he might have done something crazy like Morris in *Escape from Alcatraz*.

Based on my observations, Clint Eastwood was as out of touch with reality as most past-their-prime actors were. Every morning, he exercised

몰라 겁이 났기 때문이었다.

며칠을 겪어보니 클린트 이스트우드는 전성기가 지난 대부분의 배우들이 그렇듯 비현실적이었다. 그는 매일 아침 한 시간가량 운동을 했다. 말이 운동이지 저수지 부근을 천천히 산책하는 정도였다. 그는 항상 긴 코트와 카우보이 바지 차림이었고, 허리춤에는 실제 발사가 될까 싶을 만큼 낡은 권총까지 차고 있었다. 나는 처음에 그가 과대망상증 환자라고 생각했고, 나중에는 그래도 말을 타지 않고 맥고모자를 쓰지 않아 다행이라고 생각했다. 무섭다기보다는 창피했다. 그나마 펜션에 손님이 없는 게 다행이지 카우보이 복장의 백인 노인이 총을 소지하고 있는 것을 누가 보기라도 하면 정신이상자로 신고할 게 뻔했다. 여기는 집시가 가득한 콜로라도도, 역전의 악당이 들끓는 성 조지 요새도, 연쇄살인마가 활개를 치는 샌프란시스코도 아니었다. 뿌연 물속에 몇 마리의 민물고기가 뛰노는 저수지일 뿐이었다.

"우유 한 잔 부탁하네."

산책에서 돌아온 클린트 이스트우드가 관리실에 들어서며 말했다. 그는 무엇을 했는지 땀에 흠뻑 젖어 있었다. 나는 그에게 우유를 건넸다. 그는 우유를 받아들

for about an hour. Well, it wasn't really exercise, just walking around the reservoir. He always wore a long coat and a pair of cowboy pants. He also always kept an old gun tucked inside of his waistband. The gun was so old I doubted it was in working order. At first, I thought he might have been a megalomaniac. Later, though, I thought that it was better than him riding a horse around and wearing a straw hat. I wasn't scared of him, but embarrassed by him.

Thankfully, there were no other guests around. If anybody saw this old white man in a cowboy outfit and gun, he would have surely called the police. He wasn't in a drifter-filled Colorado anymore, or in some St. George fortress brimming with veteran villains, or in San Francisco with a serial killer at large. He was near a reservoir where only a few freshwater fish swam the muddy water.

"A glass of milk, please." Clint Eastwood said as he came in through my office on his way back from his morning walk. Whatever he did, he ended up covered in sweat. I handed him the milk. Milk in hand, he began chattering. This was his routine. I was mistaken when I'd thought he would be taciturn. Clint Eastwood babbled on and on about his life, his films, and the reasons why he had come to

고 입을 놀리기 시작했다. 그 당시 매일 겪는 일이었다. 과묵할 거라 생각했던 건 오산이었다. 클린트 이스트우드는 자신의 인생과 영화에 대해, 한국에 온 이유에 대해 설명해 나갔다. 나는 지난 열흘 동안 그 이야기를 누누이 들어 이미 다 알고 있었지만 모르는 척했다. 누군가에게 자신을 알리고 싶어 안달이 난 사람 같아서 측은했기 때문이었다.

"텍사스엔 오로지 두 종류의 음식뿐이지. 그게 뭔 줄 아나?"

그는 말을 잠시 멈추고 우유를 한 모금 마신 뒤 거드름을 피우기 시작했다. 핵심적인 대사처럼 그가 반복하는 말이었다. 나는 그의 바람대로 고개를 천천히 저어 주었다.

"소고기와 우유."

그가 목소리를 내리깔았다. 내가 먹는 음식들이 미개하다고 깔보는 듯한 기분이 들었다. 나는 겉으로는 어깨를 으쓱했지만 속으로는 더 이상 봐주기 힘든 노인네라고 투덜댔다. 그는 아랑곳하지 않고 차기작에 대한 투자를 받기 위해 여기까지 왔다고, 한 제작사와 접촉 중인데 일만 잘 풀리면 거액을 투자받을 수 있다고 떠

Korea. Although I already knew the entire story, especially after listening to him tell it for ten days, I pretended that I had no idea what he was talking about. I felt bad that he wanted so desperately to talk about himself.

"There are only two kinds of foods in Texas. Do you know what they are?" he asked haughtily after pausing in the middle of his ramblings to drink his milk. This was a question he repeated over and over like it was a famous movie line. I shook my head slowly, as I was sure he wanted.

"Beef and milk," he stated in a low voice. It seemed he was implying that the food I was eating was barbaric. I shrugged, but under my breath I muttered that I couldn't stand this old man any longer. He wasn't paying any attention to me, though, and continued to brag about how he had come here to gather investments for his next movie; he was in the midst of negotiations with a producer, and he could get an enormous sum if things went through.

"Hollywood is over," he said at some point, biting his lip. He was implying that there was no longer anybody who could recognize a master like himself in Hollywood. He also asked me if I knew that Martin Scorsese was making a 3D movie. I nodded.

드는 중이었다.

"할리우드는 이미 끝났어."

어느 순간 클린트 이스트우드가 입술을 깨물며 말했다. 자신과 같은 대가를 알아볼 안목을 갖춘 사람이 더 이상 할리우드에 존재하지 않는다는 것이었다. 그는 또 마틴 스콜세지가 3D영화를 만든다는 사실을 알고 있냐고 물었다. 나는 고개를 끄덕였다. 언젠가 기사에서 읽은 적이 있었다. 그 무렵 마틴 스콜세지의 변신은 화제가 되고 있었다.

"젊었을 때 여자를 그렇게 밝히더니 기력이 쇠한 거지. 단단히 노망이 든 게 분명해."

클린트 이스트우드가 혀를 끌끌 찼다. 그리고 "진짜 3D는 이런 거지"라고 덧붙이며 갑자기 허리춤에서 총을 꺼내 내게 겨누었다. 마틴 스콜세지가 눈앞에 있으면 쏠 기세였다. 나는 깜짝 놀라 뒤로 물러섰다.

"놀라지 말게, 젊은이. 빈총이라네. 어때? 3D처럼 실감 나지 않나?"

그가 껄껄 웃으며 총을 다시 허리춤에 찼다. 허풍쟁이 늙은이, 노망이 든 건 스콜세지가 아니라 바로 당신이야. 나는 이렇게 속으로 중얼거렸다. 그사이 클린트 이

I had read about it some time before. His transformation was the talk of the town at that time.

"He was such a womanizer when he was young. He must have lost all his mojo. He's clearly gone senile." Clint Eastwood said and clucked his tongue. Then, he added, "This is the real 3D," and removed his gun from his waistband, and aimed it at me. If Martin Scorsese had been in front of him, I thought he'd squeeze the trigger right then. I stepped back.

"Don't be alarmed, young man! It's empty." he stuck his gun back somewhere around his waist and laughed loudly. "How was it? How's that for 3D?"

What an old idiot! It's you, not Scorsese, who's gone senile! I said under my breath. Meanwhile, Clint Eastwood had stopped criticizing Martin Scorsese and had started abusing Christopher Nolan, claiming that he was all about glitzy technology without any real foundation.

"I really enjoyed his last movie, though. Didn't you?" I said. Although *The Dark Night* was a Hollywood movie, even the Cahiers du cinéma had spoken very highly of it. They said something about it being an exquisite marriage of capital and art. Shaking his head from side to side, Clint Eastwood

스트우드는 마틴 스콜세지에 대한 험담을 멈추고 기술만 번지르르할 뿐 기본이 안 됐다면서 크리스토퍼 놀란에게 욕을 퍼붓기 시작했다.

"그 영화 재밌던데요?"

내가 반문했다. 〈다크 나이트〉는 《카이에 뒤 시네마》에서도 이례적으로 극찬한 할리우드 영화였다. 자본과 예술의 절묘한 융합 운운하면서 말이다. 클린트 이스트우드는 고개를 절레절레 저으며 긴 한숨을 쉬었다. 노인의 지혜를 무시하지 말라고 충고하는 듯했다. 클린트 이스트우드는 곧이어 브라이언 드 팔마와 자신이 할리우드를 양분하던 시절에는 놀란 같은 잔챙이가 설치는 일이 없었다고, 아니 있을 수도 없는 일이었다고 말했다. 내가 알기로는 브라이언 드 팔마와 클린트 이스트우드가 할리우드를 양분하던 시절은 없었다. 그때는 그들이 조지 루카스와 스티븐 스필버그를 피해 할리우드 변방에서 저예산 괴작들을 양산하던 시기였다. 경제적으로 어려웠던 클린트 이스트우드가 돈을 벌기 위해 포르노 영화에 출연했다는 소문도 나돌고 있었다.

"이자벨 아자니에 대해서도 말해 줄까?"

클린트 이스트우드가 속삭였다. 내가 대답하기도 전

sighed deeply. He seemed to be suggesting that I shouldn't ignore the wisdom of an old man. He said that during the period when Brian de Palma and he had reigned over Hollywood, a small fish like Nolan did not, no, could not have run wild like he did these days. As far as I knew, there never really had been a time when Brian de Palma and Clint Eastwood had reigned over Hollywood. The period he was talking about was when Brian de Palma and Clint Eastwood were mass-producing low budget odd films on the margins of Hollywood, outside the influential field of George Lucas and Stephen Spielberg. There was even a rumor that Clint Eastwood had tried to solve his financial problem by acting in porno films.

"Shall I tell you about Isabelle Adjani?" whispered Clint Eastwood. Before I answered, he began to tell me how he had dated her for a while in 1981. Then, he rambled on loudly about what sexual positions she liked, how he had separated her from Daniel Day Lewis, and how her son was actually his son. Any movie fan could tell you about Isabelle Adjani's 1981 psychotic breakdown. She attempted a suicide and had been admitted to a psychiatric hospital after playing a psychopath in *Possession*. Clint Eastwood was beginning to look like an en-

에 그는 1981년 이자벨 아자니와 파리에서 만나 잠깐 사귀었다고 말했다. 그리고 이자벨 아자니가 좋아하는 체위에 대해, 다니엘 데이 루이스와 이자벨 아자니의 사이를 어떻게 갈라놓았는지에 대해, 그 둘 사이의 아들이 사실은 자신의 종자라는 것에 대해 떠벌리기 시작했다. 1981년이 이자벨 아자니가 〈포제션〉에서 사이코패스 역을 맡은 뒤 자살소동을 벌이고 정신병원에 입원한 해라는 건 영화에 조금이라도 관심이 있는 사람이라면 누구나 알고 있는 사실이다. 클린트 이스트우드는 가십난을 메우기 위해 머리를 싸매고 거짓말을 지어내는 연예부 기자 같았다. 나는 그의 허풍을 견디다 못해 그런 이야기는 한국의 정서에 맞지 않아서 듣기 불편하다고 말했다.

"〈버드〉가 막 개봉하고 난 뒤니까 아마 88년이었을 거야. LA에 머무를 때 한국 여자도 잠깐 사귀어봤어. 그녀는 코카인보다 나를 더 사랑했지. 난 그때와 다르지 않아."

그가 지나간 세월을 부정하듯 "그때와 다르지 않아."에 힘을 주어 말했다. 나는 약쟁이 교포와 한국 정서의 상관관계에 대해 잠시 생각해봤지만 그게 무엇인지 도

tertainment reporter who concocted stories in order to desperately fill up his section. At this point, I couldn't take his bragging any more and so I told him that his stories didn't suit Korean sentiments and made me feel uncomfortable.

"It was probably around 1988, since it was right after they released *Bird*. At that time I was having an affair with a Korean woman while I was staying in L.A. She loved me more than she loved cocaine. And I'm still the same person."

Clint Eastwood emphasized that last part: "I'm still the same person," as if he wanted to erase the intermediate decades between then and now.

Although I was trying hard to find a connection between the drug addicted Korean American and Korean sentiments, I couldn't understand the connection. After throwing me a few sideway glances, he stood up and said that it was time for him to go and clean his gun. He looked down at me for a while. He wasn't bragging any more. He looked as serious as Detective Callahan in *Dirty Harry*. He seemed to be accepting his current shabby situation. Then, he looked like a real fugitive. For the first time since I had met him he seemed like the real Clint Eastwood.

무지 파악할 수 없었다. 그는 내 눈치를 슬며시 보더니 이제 총을 닦으러 갈 시간이라며 자리에서 일어났다. 그는 잠깐 동안 나를 내려다보았다. 허풍을 거둬버리자 일순간 그의 눈빛이 〈더티 해리〉의 칼라한 형사처럼 진지해졌다. 자신의 초라한 신세를 인정하는 듯했다. 그러자 그가 진정한 도망자처럼 보였다. 그를 만난 후 처음으로 그가 진짜 클린트 이스트우드처럼 느껴졌다.

"마이클, 만약 당신이 우리 집 현관에 카메라를 들고 나타난다면 난 당신을 죽이겠다. 진심이다."

마이클 무어가 〈화씨 911〉을 통해 공화당을 비판하자 클린트 이스트우드는 이렇게 대응했다. 당시 마이클 무어는 클린트 이스트우드의 경고를 웃어 넘겼지만 사실은 무서워서 며칠 동안 잠을 이루지 못했다고 《버라이어티》와 인터뷰를 하는 도중 고백했다. 어린 시절 몇 번씩이나 반복해 봤던 〈석양의 건맨〉의 블론디가 총을 겨누는 꿈 때문에 뜬눈으로 밤을 지새웠다고 말이다.

그로부터 얼마 지나지 않아 마이클 무어는 할리우드 거리에서 클린트 이스트우드와 우연히 마주쳤다. 클린트 이스트우드는 무엇에 그리 쫓기는지 고개를 푹 숙인

"Michael, if you ever show up at my house with that camera, I'll shoot you on the spot. I mean it," Clint Eastwood had told Michael Moore after Moore had criticized conservatives in *Fahrenheit 911*. Although Moore laughed it off at the time, he later confessed in his interview with *Variety* that he'd so scared that he couldn't sleep for days. He said he'd a nightmare where Blondie in *The Good, the Bad, and the Ugly*, a movie he had watched many times since his childhood, was aiming right at him.

Soon afterwards, Michael Moore ran into Clint Eastwood on a street in Hollywood. Clint Eastwood was walking very quickly with his head bowed as if he was being chased. Michael Moore greeted him. He wanted to clear the air about everything that had happened rather than feel scared all the time. But Clint Eastwood just avoided him and began to walk even faster. Michael Moore said, smiling, "I felt as if I were Detective Callahan chasing some old villain. His walk and the way he acted were the same as I've seen in the movies, although that was the first time I'd seen him act as if he was afraid and run away like that. He was moving so fast that he disappeared before I could even try to catch up to him." Michael Moore seemed oddly triumphant. The reporter asked if he was sure that it had been

채 빠른 걸음으로 걷고 있었다. 마이클 무어는 클린트 이스트우드에게 인사를 건넸다. 공포에 떠느니 빨리 상황에 부딪혀 이겨내는 게 낫다는 생각에서였다. 그러나 클린트 이스트우드는 마이클 무어를 피해 더 빨리 걷기 시작했다. 마이클 무어는 "악당을 쫓는 칼라한 형사가 된 기분이었죠"라고 운을 떼며 "걸음걸이나 행동거지 모두 어린 시절 영화에서 봤던 그대로였어요. 겁에 질린 듯 도망가는 모습은 처음이었지만요. 얼마나 빠른지 순식간에 사라지더라고요"라고 웃음을 머금은 채 말했다. 자신이 최후의 승자라는 태도였다. 기자는 클린트 이스트우드가 확실하냐고 물었다.

"처음에는 저도 헷갈렸어요. 미국에서 흔히 볼 수 있는, 그러니까 무료함을 이기지 못해 평생교육원에서 시 창작이나 배우고 온 듯한 노인이었거든요. 그러나 클린트 이스트우드가 분명하다는 확신은 있었죠. 어떻게 제가 그를 잊을 리 있나요. 어릴 때는 우상이었고 요새는 꿈마다 나오는데 말이죠."

마이클 무어는 이렇게 덧붙이곤 자신이 본 게 클린트 이스트우드든 아니든 이제 미국의 부흥기를 이끌었던 기성세대들이 서서히 사라질 때라고 말했다. 〈석양의

Clint Eastwood.

"I was also a little confused at first. He looked like one of those old men just out of some poetry writing class at a community education center he'd taken just out of boredom. But I was sure that it was Clint Eastwood. How could I not recognize Clint Eastwood? He was my childhood hero and lately I saw him every night in my dreams," Michael Moore added.

Moore then argued that, whether the person he had seen was Clint Eastwood or not, it was now time for the older generation who had led the golden age of American cinema to retire. He said it as if he was Lee Van Cleef, who played Clint Eastwood's archenemy in *The Good, the Bad, and the Ugly*.

What he argued wasn't necessarily wrong. *Mystic River*, *Changeling*, and *Gran Torino* were critical successes and production companies used epithets like "The last classicist of our time" to describe Clint Eastwood's movies. Financially, though, these movies couldn't even pass the break-even point. Without mega-capital, special effects, or famous actors, this wasn't surprising. Although he reconciled with ethnic minorities in *Hereafter* and had tried to change his movie world by exploring space

무법자〉에서 클린트 이스트우드의 숙적으로 나오는 리반 클리프라도 된 것처럼 말이다. 틀린 말은 아니었다. 〈미스틱 리버〉와 〈체인질링〉과 〈그랜토리노〉가 연이어 평단의 호평을 받고 영화사들은 "우리 시대의 마지막 고전주의자" 같은 수식어를 붙였지만 사실 그 영화들은 하나같이 손익분기점을 넘지 못했다. 거대자본과 특수효과도 없었고 유명 배우가 출연하는 게 아니었으니 당연했다. 〈히어애프터〉에서 소수민족과 화해하고 〈스페이스 카우보이〉를 통해 우주 공간을 모색하며 변화를 꾀했지만 40년 이상을 할리우드에서 버티기엔 강인한 육체만으론 역부족이었다. 게다가 육체는 점점 노쇠했고 퇴물이 된 여배우처럼 과거 속에 매몰돼 현실을 직시하지 못했다. 더군다나 제작자와의 다툼으로 인해 할리우드에 더 이상 발을 붙일 수 없었다. 내 영웅이 이렇게 망가지다니…… 차라리 나타나질 말지…… 나는 문득 서글퍼졌다. 이건 호르몬보다 좀더 불가항력적인 문제임에 틀림없었다.

그럼에도 나는 클린트 이스트우드를 봐줄 수 없었다. 그가 펜션에 온 뒤 혼자 영화 보는 시간을 빼앗겼기 때문이었다. 그는 관리실에 시도 때도 없이 드나들었고

in *Space Cowboys*, even his robust body couldn't sustain him for more than forty years in Hollywood. Besides, his body was growing old as well. Submerged in his splendid past, he couldn't face reality like an obsolete old actress staring down at hers. Additionally, he could no longer remain in Hollywood because of his frequent quarrels with producers. How could my hero have fallen apart like this? I wished that he hadn't shown up at my guesthouse. Suddenly, I felt sad. His problem must have been due to something fateful, much bigger than just hormones.

Nevertheless, I couldn't stand Clint Eastwood. I had lost my solitary time of watching movies since he'd arrived in the guesthouse. He frequented my office as he pleased, and spoke ill of actors while I watched movies. According to him, Dustin Hoffman was an Italian country bumpkin who only knew about tomato sauce; half of Alain Delon's fans were gay; Paul Newman was shameless and had no basic ethical values; and Al Pacino and Robert De Niro were too young to even compare to himself.

He even belittled John Wayne: "John Wayne was an impossible old man." He didn't want to have anything to do with Asian movies. When I watched contemporary action films like *The Bourne Identity*,

영화를 보는 도중 끼어들어 배우들의 험담을 해대기 일쑤였다. 그의 말에 따르면 더스틴 호프만은 토마토소스밖에 모르는 이탈리아 촌놈이고, 알랭 들롱의 팬은 절반이 동성애자인 데다가, 폴 뉴먼은 최소한의 윤리관도 없는 작자이며, 알 파치노와 로버트 드 니로는 자신과 같은 급이라고 하기엔 새까만 후배들이었다.

"존 웨인 그 노인네는 대책 없는 꼰대야."

심지어 그는 존 웨인을 깎아내리기도 했다. 그는 동양 영화들은 취급도 하지 않았으며 〈본 아이덴티티〉 같은 현대물을 볼 때는 "총은 저렇게 쏘는 게 아니야"라고 트집을 잡으며 총을 꺼내 시범을 보이기도 했다. 그를 내쫓는 방법은 간단했다. 지루한 영화를 트는 것이다.

"영화를 이렇게 고리타분하게 만들다니. 그 나이 먹도록 영화 만드는 법을 모르는군."

데이비드 린치의 영화를 틀면 클린트 이스트우드는 이렇게 말하며 하품을 했다. 예전 같았으면 그 말에 어느 정도 동의를 하며 고개를 끄덕였겠지만, 유일한 취미 생활마저 빼앗겨버린 나는 괜한 반발심이 생겼던 것 같다. 그 덕에 린치의 영화를 몇 번이나 반복해 봤는지 모르겠다. 그중 몇 장면은 아직도 머릿속에서 사라지지

he'd said, "That's not how you shoot," and took out his gun to show me how to shoot correctly. It was easy to kick him out of my office, though. All I had to do was to play something boring.

"Terrible! At his age, he still doesn't know how to make a movie." This was what he said when I'd played a David Lynch film. He was yawning. In the beginning I might have agreed and nodded. But I was upset because my only hobby had been taken away. I ended up watching David Lynch's movie over and over again. I still remember a number of scenes from his movies.

"Have you seen my movies?" he asked. He mentioned Sergio Leone's Western and Don Siegel's *Coogan's Bluff*; he seemed to be suggesting that I should watch movies where he'd played the protagonist. But I did not feel like watching them in front of him. I not only hated even to imagine how he'd act in front of those old movies but I also felt sorry for him since they could be reminders of his current fallen status. I almost felt angry towards Brecht, who had come up with the notion of the "alienation effect." What on earth was a film if not an illusion? Why wasn't the Clint Eastwood who was right in front of me the real Clint Eastwood?

So I watched movies only after he went to bed.

않는다.

“내 영화는 봤나?”

그는 한술 더 떠서 세르지오 레오네의 서부극이나 돈 시겔의 〈일망타진〉을 언급하며 은근히 자신의 영화를 틀길 바랐다. 그러나 그의 앞에서 그 영화들을 본다는 게 내키지 않았다. 우쭐해하는 그가 상상돼 싫기도 했지만 그의 처지를 확인 사살하는 것 같아 왠지 미안한 마음도 들었기 때문이었다. 소격효과를 창안한 브레히트가 원망스러울 지경이었다. 영화가 환상이 아니라면 대체 무엇이란 말인가. 어째서 눈앞에 있는 클린트 이스트우드가 진짜 클린트 이스트우드란 말인가.

그러니 영화를 보는 시간은 주로 클린트 이스트우드가 잠들고 나서였다. 그렇다고 완전히 그의 사격 범위에서 벗어난 건 아니었다. 언젠가 한번은 새벽에 관리실 문을 두드린 적도 있었다.

“혹시 내 앞으로 전화나 편지 안 왔나?”

그가 관리실 문을 벌컥 열며 말했다. 착각하지 마세요. 당신은 이제 지역 신문에서도 찾아보기 힘들어요. 동네 잡화점 주인 할아버지의 부고에도 밀릴 지경이라고요. 나는 이렇게 속으로 중얼거렸다. 실제로도 그의

That did not mean, though, I was completely out of his range. Once he knocked on the door of my office at dawn, burst in, and said: "Were there any phone calls or letters for me?"

Wake up, old man! Your name is almost impossible to find even in community newsletters now. A grocery store owner's obituary takes precedence over you. I muttered things like that under my breath. In fact, the news of his hiding out had been completely forgotten, pushed back by the scandals of much younger actors. Police officers had most likely set aside their pursuit of him. They were busy solving more important cases. Michael Moore must have overcome his fear of Clint Eastwood. He had just released *Sicko*, which was well received critically. Clint Eastwood was a clumsy fugitive who didn't quite understand his situation.

"They always found me wherever I went into hiding in the old days," he complained.

I almost said, "Would you like me to report you to the police?" But I didn't want to give him an opportunity to ramble. Instead, I just kicked him out after giving him a glass of milk. He went back to his room after pacing back and forth outside of my office, wearing the depressed look of a would-be actor who had just failed his audition.

도주 사건은 젊은 배우들의 스캔들에 밀려 잊힌 지 오래였다. 경찰도 연일 몰려드는 중요한 사건을 해결하느라 그를 추격하는 것을 미뤄놓았을 것이었다. 마이클 무어는 클린트 이스트우드에 대한 공포를 극복했는지 〈식코〉를 만들어 평단의 호평을 받았다. 클린트 이스트우드는 아직도 상황 파악을 제대로 하지 못한 얼치기 도망자였다.

"예전엔 내가 그 어떤 곳에 숨어 있어도 잘도 찾아내더니만."

그가 투덜거렸다. 나는 그럼 신고라도 해드려요? 하고 말하려다가 참았다. 그의 이야기가 길어질까 겁났기 때문이었다. 나는 우유 한 잔을 주어 그를 내쫓았다. 그는 오디션에 탈락해 낙담한 배우 지망생처럼 침울한 표정으로 한동안 밖을 서성이다가 방으로 들어갔다.

나는 일주일에 서너 번 저수지에 배를 띄워 물 위에 떠오른 오물을 건져내는 일을 했다. 클린트 이스트우드는 그때마다 눈치 없이 따라나서며 나를 귀찮게 했다.

"리오그란데 강이 떠오르네."

시커먼 저수지를 한동안 내려다보던 클린트 이스트우드가 입을 열었다. 그리고 리오그란데를 배경으로 한

A few times every week, I went out to the reservoir on the boat to clean up the trash floating on the surface. Every time Clint Eastwood followed me out to the boat, making himself a nuisance all the while.

"This reminds me of the Rio Grande," Clint Eastwood said after looking down the river quietly. He began to tell me the history of the Western, set against the backdrop of the Rio Grande. His story began with John Ford and went back to the story of the American War of Independence, dozens of fights against Indians populating his story along the way. Then, suddenly, his story stopped. He didn't seem to know the contemporary reality that Indians and Americans weren't fighting over territory and pride anymore, but over the pockets of tourists the Rio Grande attracted after it had been developed as a tourist attraction in the Reagan era.

"Well, both this reservoir and the Rio Grande are dirty," I said brusquely, and drew my net in. Pieces of fur-covered Styrofoam were caught in the net.

"I used to write scenarios in hotel rooms while I looked out at the Rio Grande. The sandstorms whirling over the Rio Grande were so inspiring," he said. His eyes were half closed as if he was facing down a sandstorm at that very moment. "But when

서부극의 역사에 대해 설명하기 시작했다. 존 포드에서 시작한 그 이야기는 독립전쟁 당시 리오그란데에서 하루에도 열두 번씩 인디언들과 전투를 벌였다는 이야기까지 거슬러 올라가다가 어느 순간 끝나버렸다. 레이건 정권 때부터 관광지로 개발된 리오그란데에서 인디언과 백인이 영토와 자존심이 아니라 관광객의 주머니를 두고 다투는 현실을 모르고 있는 듯했다.

"더러운 건 피차일반이죠."

나는 시큰둥하게 답하며 망을 건져 올렸다. 물때가 낀 스티로폼 조각들이 망에 걸려 있었다.

"리오그란데가 내다보이는 호텔에서 시나리오를 쓰곤 했다네. 리오그란데를 휘감는 사막의 모래바람을 보고 있으면 영감이 저절로 떠올랐지."

모래바람을 만난 듯 그가 눈을 가늘게 뜨며 말했다.

"글을 쓰다가 강 너머 멕시코를 바라보면 인디언들의 지독한 구취가 풍겨오는 거 같은 기분이 들어 영감이 금세 사라졌지만 말이야."

그가 미간을 잔뜩 찌푸리며 덧붙였다. 〈무법자 조시 웨일즈〉에서 보여준 코만치족과의 화합은 그저 영화를 팔기 위한 수단에 불과했다고 말하는 듯했다. 나는 그

I looked across the river at Mexico, my inspiration seemed to dissolve instantly."

"I could almost smell the foul breath of Indians blowing over the water," he added, furrowing his forehead severely. He seemed to be implying that reconciling with the Comanches in *The Outlaw Josey Wales* was just a narrative ploy to sell movie tickets.

Not paying too much attention to what he was saying, I put the trash I had just picked up into a trash bag. I didn't have much to say to him, and besides that, I didn't have the heart to interfere with his memories. At some point, after staring out at the reservoir for a while, he began to tear up. He looked so old and weak. He looked like even if I had tied him up and pushed him out of the boat he'd be unable to fight back.

"So you're a writer, too, huh?" he asked.

I said, "I guess so," and nodded.

"What a pathetic profession!" He continued, smiling sardonically. "It's worse than being a pimp with leprosy."

He began to laugh loudly. Suddenly, I wanted to push him into the water. I regretted pitying him even for a moment. He stopped laughing and chattering about things about Texas. Meanwhile, I was trying to figure out which director would be the

의 이야기를 흘려들으며 망에 걸린 쓰레기를 봉투에 넣었다. 달리 할 말이 없기도 했지만 그의 회상을 방해할 만큼 나는 모질지 못했다. 어느 순간부터 말을 멈추고 한동안 저수지를 바라보던 그의 눈망울이 촉촉해지기 시작했다. 그는 포박한 뒤 뱃머리에서 밀어버린다 해도 아무런 저항도 못 할 것처럼 쇠약해 보였다.

"그래, 자네도 글을 쓴다고 했지?"

그때 그가 물었다. 나는 "그런 셈이죠"라고 대답하며 고개를 끄덕였다.

"나약하기 짝이 없는 직업이군."

그가 비웃음을 띠며 말을 이었다.

"문둥병에 걸린 포주만도 못한 직업이지."

그가 소리 내 웃기 시작했다. 불현듯 그를 물속에 떠밀고 싶어졌다. 잠시나마 그를 동정한 게 후회됐다. 그가 웃음을 멈추고 텍사스 운운하며 다시 헛소리를 늘어놓는 동안 나는 상상 속에서 그를 빠뜨릴 지시를 내릴 감독을 고르고 있었다. 샘 페킨파는 너무 잔인한가…… 데이비드 크로넨버그라면 그나마 멋스럽게 그려줄 테고…… 조지 로메로라면 실제로도 죽이는 게 가능할까?

best to direct his drowning scene. Would Sam Peckinpah be too cruel? David Cronenberg would depict it pretty stylishly... Perhaps, George Romero would actually kill him?

Around that time, I visited my uncle at the nursing home in Hongseong, Chungnam once every other week. His doctor had told me that he didn't have much time left.

One day, I went to see him and found myself waiting for him in the meeting room. The wisteria trees shaded the yard adjacent to the meeting room. I could see the jagged cliffs of mountains beyond the yard. A short while later, a nurse arrived wheeling my uncle in. He looked hale and hearty, perhaps emanating his life's last fires.

"How's the guesthouse?" he asked as soon as he saw me. It was as if his life's only achievement was that guesthouse. I told him the guesthouse was fine.

"How many guests are staying there now?" my uncle asked. There was only one, I said. Suddenly, I became worried. What if Clint Eastwood, left alone in the guesthouse, had kidnapped someone and was making a scene?

"Make sure to treat all the travelers well," Uncle

그 무렵 나는 2주에 한 번꼴로 충남 홍성에 위치한 요양원에 다녀왔다. 주치의에게 숙부가 오래지 않아 죽을 거란 말을 들어서였다. 나는 면회 신청을 한 뒤 마당에서 숙부를 기다렸다. 면회실 마당에는 등나무들이 그늘을 드리우며 늘어서 있었고, 마당 너머 암석이 적나라하게 드러난 산이 보였다. 얼마 지나지 않아 간호사가 휠체어에 탄 숙부를 밀고 나왔다. 숙부는 삶의 마지막 빛을 발하는 듯 정정해 보였다.

"펜션은?"

숙부는 나를 보자마자 펜션에 대해 물었다. 평생을 걸려 얻은 게 그 펜션 하나뿐이라는 듯이. 나는 펜션은 잘 있다고 대답했다.

"지금 몇 명이 묵고 있지?"

숙부가 재차 물었다. 나는 한 명이 묵고 있다고 답했다. 문득 펜션에 혼자 남은 클린트 이스트우드가 누군가를 납치해 와 인질극이라도 벌이고 있는 게 아닐까 불안해졌다.

"나그네에게 대접 잘해주게."

숙부는 이렇게 말하곤 쓸쓸한 얼굴로 돌산을 바라봤

said, and stared out at the mountains, a lonely look on his face. For a second, he looked like the traveler, a lone traveler preparing for his final journey. I felt like I had to say something comforting.

"Do you like Clint Eastwood?" The words just came out of my mouth. My uncle said nothing to this, as if still lost in thoughts about his life's journey.

"As far as I know, he was the coolest man I'd ever seen," my uncle said, quietly. He seemed to have finally finished looking back on his life. He began excitedly telling me some mundane stories about how he used to go to double-feature special theaters then. I listened politely.

Interestingly, his stories stopped at *Unforgiven*, the climax of Clint Eastwood's career. He had made a comeback with this movie, receiving Academy Awards in the categories of Best Picture and Best Director after years of lackluster performance as a director. *Unforgiven* was a Western that had depicted the end of the Western film, all based on Eastwood's own experiences. In the movie, he'd played the role of an ex-gunman and, at one point, he confesses the pain of a gunman and exposes the true reality of Western heroism. Cruelly, he had only one chance to reflect on himself. Uncle didn't

다. 나는 숙부가 도리어 영영 떠나버릴 준비를 하는 나그네란 생각이 들었고, 그의 기분을 풀어줘야겠다는 생각도 들었다.

"클린트 이스트우드 좋아하세요?"

나도 모르게 튀어나온 말이었다. 숙부는 인생을 돌이켜보듯 한동안 침묵을 지켰다.

"내가 아는 한 최고의 남자였지."

숙부가 숙고를 끝낸 듯 차분한 목소리로 말했다. 그리곤 클린트 이스트우드의 영화를 보기 위해 동시상영관에 드나들던 고리타분한 이야기를 신이 나서 쏟아내기 시작했다. 나는 숙부의 이야기를 잠자코 들어주었다. 이야기는 신기하게도 클린트 이스트우드의 정점인 〈용서받지 못한 자〉에서 멈췄다. 감독으로서 한동안 죽을 쑤던 클린트 이스트우드는 〈용서받지 못한 자〉로 아카데미 작품상과 감독상을 동시에 수상하며 재기에 성공했다. 〈용서받지 못한 자〉는 클린트 이스트우드 자신을 재료 삼아 서부극의 종말을 형상화한 영화였다. 퇴물 총잡이로 분한 클린트 이스트우드가 총잡이의 고통을 토로하고 서부 영웅주의의 실체를 폭로한 것이다. 그러나 자신을 반영할 수 있는 기회는 잔인하게도 단 한 번

seem to know about Clint Eastwood's downturn since then. After finishing his stories, Uncle began to cough. It seemed that he had become too excited and had talked too much. He probably wanted to prove that he had also had splendid youthful years. I didn't tell him that Clint Eastwood was now hiding out in his guesthouse. Even a complete villain wouldn't shatter the illusions of a dying man.

"I remember how women all went crazy when *The Red Circle* was released," Uncle mused. "Anyway, is he still alive?"

I felt something was wrong, and then realized that the hero in *The Red Circle* hadn't been Clint Eastwood, but Alain Delon. I didn't correct him. Nothing would change if Uncle died without knowing the truth.

I dropped by the movie magazine office on my way back to the guesthouse. I wanted to show a former colleague the movie premise I had been working on for a while. He was busy trying to meet deadlines for a newly released movie review. I handed him my premise and he began skimming through it. But he put it down pretty quickly. He hadn't read even half of it. His advice was candid. He asked me how I thought such a simple narrative would sell and he said that he wasn't surprised that

뿐이었다. 그다음의 내리막길에 대해서 숙부는 모르는 듯했다. 이야기를 마치자 숙부가 기침을 하기 시작했다. 자신에게도 찬란한 젊은 시절이 있었다는 듯 갑자기 흥분해 너무 많은 이야기를 쏟아낸 듯했다. 나는 숙부에게 클린트 이스트우드가 펜션에 숨어 있다는 말을 하지 않았다. 곧 죽는 사람의 환상을 깨는 건 아무리 악랄한 악당도 못 할 짓이다.

"〈암흑가의 세 사람〉이 개봉했을 때 여자들이 열광했던 게 기억나네. 그나저나 그 양반 아직 살아 있나?"

숙부가 병실에 들어가기 전에 말했다. 곰곰이 생각해보니 무언가 이상했다. 〈암흑가의 세 사람〉에 출연한 건 클린트 이스트우드가 아니라 알랭 들롱이었다. 나는 입을 다물었다. 알고 죽으나 모르고 죽으나 변하는 건 없으니까.

펜션으로 돌아가는 길에 아직 영화잡지 기자로 있는 동료에게 들렀다. 시나리오를 보여주기 위해서였다. 동료는 마감이 코앞이라며 개봉 영화 평을 쓰느라 정신이 없었고 시나리오를 건네자 건성으로 훑어보기 시작했다. 얼마 지나지 않아 그는 시나리오를 내려놓았다. 절반도 읽지 않은 채였다. 그는 이렇게 서사가 단순하면

my scenario hadn't won. I took a quick look at the review he was writing. It was a review of an average disaster movie. He was drawing upon all kinds of theories to praise it. For whatever reason he must have liked it. Since I confirmed his critical talent, I felt better, although I still felt a bit bitter. He seemed to have forgotten about Jean Luc Goddard and Alain Resnais.

"I hope you aren't still only watching those gunfighting movies," he noted wryly. He, then, mentioned the names of several up and coming European and American directors—names even hard to remember—and said that they were opening new horizons for movies. I told him that I hadn't heard of any of them. He shook his head and said that I was still caught in the past.

"Do you know what the most popular name is in Texas?" he asked me, grinning. I shook my head.

"Clint Eastwood," he said.

Then, he asked, "What name do you think these Clint Eastwoods hate the most?" I shook my head again.

"Clint Eastwood," he said again. Then, he began to giggle, as if he had just said something hilarious. He said he had just read this joke in a magazine column. According to the column, there were an

팔릴 리가 있냐고, 공모전에서 떨어지는 게 당연하다고 쓴소리를 해댔다. 나는 그가 쓴 평을 흘끗 봤다. 요즘 개봉한 그저 그런 재난영화에 대한 평이었는데, 동료는 뭐가 그리 좋은지 온갖 이론을 끌어들여 찬사하고 있었다. 나는 그의 감식안을 확인한 뒤 안심하는 한편 씁쓸하기도 했다. 동료는 장 뤽 고다르와 알랭 레네마저 잊어버린 듯했다.

"아직도 무작정 총싸움하는 영화만 보는 건 아니겠지?"

동료가 비아냥댔다. 그리곤 이름도 외우기 힘든 서양의 젊은 감독들을 대며 그들이 영화의 새 지평을 열고 있다고 말했다. 나는 그들을 모른다고 했다. 동료는 고개를 절레절레 저으며 내가 과거에 붙잡혀 있는 사람이라고 말했다.

"텍사스에서 가장 흔한 이름이 뭔 줄 알아?"

동료가 히죽히죽 웃으며 물었다. 나는 고개를 저었다.

"클린트 이스트우드."

동료가 말했다.

"그럼 클린트 이스트우드들이 가장 증오하는 이름은?"

especially large amount of Clint Eastwoods among the youth in Texas, and they all hated their own ridiculous names, wondering why their grandmother had done it.

"That's reality. So, why are you so eager to become Clint Eastwood?" He was getting on my nerves. In fact, at that very moment I was imagining Clint Eastwood was aiming at him from afar with his signature Winchester.

I arrived at the guesthouse after midnight. When I entered my office, I found Clint Eastwood inside watching a movie. It was *Subway*, the movie where Isabelle Adjani played the heroine. It was a movie that deserved worship just for Isabelle Adjani's beautiful acting. *Subway* wasn't a sad movie. It was a crime movie, if my memory was correct. But Clint Eastwood was crying, not even aware that I'd entered the office. I felt awkward, and I just stood there. Clint Eastwood must have sensed my presence then. He quickly turned off the TV and stumbled to his feet like a teenage boy caught watching porn.

"I hope everything's all right," I said, softly. Clint Eastwood was looking at me as if he had something to tell me, his eyes still brimming with tears.

"How was the movie?" I asked, trying to break

나는 또 고개를 저었다.

"클린트 이스트우드."

동료가 또 말했다. 그리고 아주 우스운 농담을 한 듯 낄낄대기 시작했다. 얼마 전 어느 칼럼에서 읽은 우스갯소리인데, 이제 막 청년이 된 텍사스의 젊은이들 중에는 유난히 클린트 이스트우드라는 이름을 가진 사람이 많다는 것이었다. 클린트 이스트우드들은 "왜 할머니가 이런 이름을 지어줬는지 모르겠어요"라고 말하며 자신의 우스꽝스러운 이름을 하나같이 증오한다고 한다.

"근데 너는 왜 클린트 이스트우드가 되지 못해 안달이지?"

동료가 이죽거렸다. 나는 그때 클린트 이스트우드가 저 멀리서 윈체스터로 동료를 저격하는 상상을 했던 것 같다.

펜션에 도착했을 때는 자정이 넘어서였다. 관리실에 들어가자 클린트 이스트우드가 영화를 보고 있었다. 이자벨 아자니가 나오는 〈서브웨이〉였다. 이자벨 아자니의 아름다운 모습만으로도 추앙받아야 마땅한 영화였다. 내 기억이 맞다면 〈서브웨이〉는 그다지 슬프지 않은 범죄물인데도 클린트 이스트우드는 내가 옆에 다가온

the uncomfortable silence.

"I'm actually not really that great of a celebrity... past my prime... I'm pathetic, really." His voice was low, as if he was confessing something. He added, scornfully. "Weeping over my first love."

I stood still, not knowing what to say. He began to stumble out of my office. At the same time, I realized a drawer near where he was standing was slightly open. There had been a small amount of money and my manuscripts in it. I watched him disappear. I could see a few notes peeking out from his coat pocket. I realized that it was time for him to pay his fee and that the money in the drawer was far short of the amount he owed. A gunman turned into a petty thief? What the heck had happened?

Although I pretended not to have noticed, Clint Eastwood kept avoiding me. At some point, he also began to go out after his morning stroll. Knowing his financial situation, I didn't feel like giving him a hard time about his debt. I also preferred not seeing him.

Besides, I was too busy revising my movie pitch to pay attention to him. I also saw all the movies by the young directors my former colleague had men-

것도 모른 채 눈물을 흘리고 있었다. 나는 당황해서 그 자리에 멈췄다. 그는 그때서야 인기척을 느꼈는지 포르노 영화를 보다 들킨 소년처럼 후다닥 텔레비전을 끄고 일어섰다.

“별일 없었죠?”

내가 괜히 민망해져 물었다. 클린트 이스트우드는 눈물 고인 눈으로 나를 보며 무슨 할 말이라도 있는 듯 입을 달싹였다.

“영화는 어땠어요?”

불편한 침묵을 끝내고자 내가 다시 한 번 물었다.

“난 사실 그리 유명한 사람이 아니네. 전성기도 지났고…… 첫사랑을 떠올리며 훌쩍대는 나약한 남자일 뿐이지.”

클린트 이스트우드가 고백이라도 하듯 나직한 목소리로 말했다. 나는 갑작스런 고백에 멀거니 서 있을 수밖에 없었다. 그러자 그는 슬며시 자리에서 일어나 밖으로 나갔다. 그때 나는 그가 빠져나간 자리에 놓인 서랍장이 살짝 열려 있는 것을 발견했다. 얼마간의 돈과 시나리오 습작들이 담긴 서랍이었다. 나는 관리실을 빠져나가는 그를 바라보았다. 그의 코트 주머니에는 지폐

tioned. But because they had too many layers, it was hard to understand their themes. Also, they were so preoccupied with lush visuals that I felt exhausted by the time I finished watching them. The new world of movies had become so complicated that a *Dirty Harry* catchphrase like "Go ahead, make my day" would never have worked in any of them.

In this artistic climate, it wasn't surprising that the Western had disappeared almost entirely. Early Westerns had more traditional, archetypal structures—the pseudo-mythic narrative, heroic characters, white supremacist ideals, and Manichean good vs. evil formulas. Although the Western had tried to survive by allying itself with non-whites and embracing women, these efforts had not been enough. As if by magic, the Western had suddenly found itself wiped out. Some critics validated this end of the Western, mentioning embryonic defects, etc. But my opinion was different. The Western hadn't died. The Western was closely related to each phase of our reality, from the frontier era through the Vietnam War, from Capitalism and the Cold War system to Marxism, Nazism, and Mussolini. The spirit of the Western was still alive in our contemporary world. It was we who were stagger-

몇 장이 삐져나와 있었다. 나는 그때서야 클린트 이스트우드가 숙박비를 지불할 때가 됐다는 것을 깨달았고, 서랍 안에 있는 돈이 숙박비를 내기엔 턱없이 부족한 금액이라는 것도 깨달았다. 건맨이 좀도둑이 되다니…… 정녕 무슨 문제란 말인가?

돈을 훔친 걸 모른 척해준 이후 클린트 이스트우드는 나를 슬슬 피해 다녔다. 그리고 언제부턴가 아침 산책을 한 뒤 외출하기 시작했다. 처지를 아는 마당에 숙박비를 내라고 닦달하기도 왠지 좀 그래서 나 역시 그를 보지 않는 게 편했다. 게다가 시나리오를 고치느라 좀처럼 그에게 신경을 쓰지 못했다. 동료가 말한 젊은 감독들의 영화도 연달아 봤는데, 몇 겹의 서사 구조를 갖고 있어서 도무지 주제를 파악하기 힘들었고 하나같이 화려한 화면에만 집착할 뿐이어서 영화를 보고 나면 지쳐버렸다. 〈더티 해리〉의 명대사 "오늘 하루를 화끈하게 장식해줘."가 통하지 않을 만큼 영화를 둘러싼 세계는 복잡해진 상태였다. 이런 맥락에서 보면 서부극이 사라진 건 당연했다. 초창기 서부극은 신화 위조, 영웅주의, 백인우월주의, 단순한 선악 구도처럼 확연히 드러나는

ing without any context, or maybe caught within the network of too many contexts, as if we had been hypnotized.

Watching those movies my former colleague had recommended to me night after night, I suddenly began to miss those guys wandering endlessly through the desert as if possessed by ghosts. I even missed Clint Eastwood, who hadn't been back in his room for three days. It was as if he'd intentionally decided not to come back so that I would end up missing him. For a moment, I really did feel like he would never return. That must have been why I went inside his room. I sometimes imagined that his room would look like one of those shabby hamlets you see in so many Westerns. Disappointingly, however, his room was exactly the same as the other rooms in that guesthouse. On top of his small desk was John Steinbeck's *Grapes of Wrath*. There was no gun lying around, so he must have taken it. I could imagine Clint Eastwood making a scene with an empty gun and a cowboy outfit. It reminded me of Jacques Tati's comedies where he used the device of the naïve gentleman, like Monsieur Hulot, to satirize modern society. I began to clean up his room. It wasn't hard, because the room was relatively clean and there wasn't too

단점이 많았다. 그 이후 서부극은 유색인종과 연대하고 여성을 보듬으며 살아남으려 버둥댔지만 그것만으로는 부족했다. 그러던 중 서부극은 유령에 홀린 듯 순식간에 사라졌다. 일부 평자들은 태생적 한계를 운운하며 서부극의 종말을 정당화했다. 그러나 내 생각은 달랐다. 서부극은 사라지지 않았다. 서부개척시대와 베트남전쟁, 자본주의와 냉전체제, 마르크스와 나치와 무솔리니까지 서부극은 당시 현실과 맥락이 닿아 있고 그 정신은 현재까지 유효했다. 내 생각엔 우리가 오히려 아무 맥락 없이, 혹은 너무나 많은 맥락에 닿아 최면에 걸린 것처럼 비틀거릴 뿐이었다. 밤새 동료가 권한 영화를 보고 있자니 나는 문득 유령에 홀린 채 끝없이 사막을 헤매고 있는 남자들이 그리워졌다. 클린트 이스트우드마저 보고 싶은 생각이 들었다. 그 무렵 내 그리움을 자극하려고 하는지 클린트 이스트우드는 사흘 동안 들어오지 않았다. 그때 나는 직감적으로 그가 영영 돌아오지 않을 거라 생각했던 것 같다. 그것밖에는 그의 방에 들어간 이유가 설명되지 않는다.

나는 가끔 클린트 이스트우드가 방을 서부극에 나오는 허름한 오두막처럼 꾸며놓지는 않았을까 상상하곤

much stuff. Everything he owned could fit in his one suitcase.

Betraying my expectations, Clint Eastwood returned the next afternoon. He came with a young woman I had never seen before.

"How are you?" Clint Eastwood greeted me. I told him that I had packed his luggage, thinking that he had left.

"Where would I go?" he asked triumphantly. He looked absolutely self-confident. I took a side-glance at the woman arm in arm with him. Only then did Clint Eastwood introduce us to each other. I can't remember now what her name was or how they met. The only thing I remember was that she was a hooker.

"Since I have a lady guest this evening, how about a steak?" he said, and gave me a wad of money, adding that he'd gotten a down payment from a movie company. It looked like that wad of money was what was making him so cocky. After setting aside the amount he owed for his stay, I bought meat with the rest of money. While I was cooking the steak, the couple drank beer and chatted on the terrace. I had to admit that Clint Eastwood was a natural actor. I watched them talking. It was a completely captivating scene. It was as if I was

했다. 그러나 허무하게도 그의 방은 펜션의 다른 방들과 똑같았다. 자그마한 탁상 위에 존 스타인벡의 『분노의 포도』가 놓여 있을 뿐이었다. 총은 갖고 나갔는지 보이지 않았다. 나는 빈총과 카우보이 복장으로 희극적인 광경을 연출할 클린트 이스트우드를 떠올렸다. 어리숙한 신사 윌로 씨를 등장시켜 현대사회를 풍자하는 자크 타티의 코미디 같았다. 나는 방을 정리하기 시작했다. 방도 비교적 깨끗했고 짐도 가방 하나 분량이어서 힘들지는 않았다.

다음 날 늦은 오후였다. 예상은 빗나갔다. 클린트 이스트우드가 돌아온 것이다. 처음 보는 젊은 여자와 함께였다.

"잘 있었나?"

클린트 이스트우드가 내게 인사를 건넸다. 나는 당신이 떠난 줄 알고 방을 치운 뒤 짐을 따로 챙겨뒀다고 말했다.

"내가 어디 가나?"

그가 우쭐대며 말했다. 자신감이 넘쳐 보였다. 나는 그의 팔짱을 끼고 있는 여자를 곁눈질했다. 클린트 이스트우드는 그때서야 우리 둘을 서로 소개해 주었다.

watching a scene in *The Bridges of Madison County*. Soon the woman went to the bathroom and Clint Eastwood came over to me, staggering and swaying back and forth.

"There's no arguing that nothing goes better with a stiff drink than a woman," Clint Eastwood said. "Isn't she pretty?"

He reeked of alcohol. I didn't answer. He began to talk about all the women he'd been with. I can't remember all the names, but they certainly included all manner of famous actresses.

"Your movie premise was enjoyable, but it... it lacked something," he suddenly said, his expression serious. It was then that I realized that he had read my movie pitch without asking for my permission. In retrospect, I realized that he had not been wide off the mark. I might have imitated some movies, but I didn't have any clear conflicts like racial conflicts or the Vietnam War. This wasn't an excuse, of course. Anyway, I thought that Clint Eastwood might have run away from Hollywood for the same reason I had. I almost felt a sort of camaraderie with him. Still, I felt upset. I regretted that I had ever missed Clint Eastwood, even for a couple of days. I wondered if I would be forever fading away together with him in this world. I felt

지금은 그녀가 창녀였다는 것 말고는 그들이 어디에서 만났는지 그녀의 이름이 무엇인지 기억나지 않는다.

"숙녀가 왔는데 오늘 저녁은 스테이크 어떤가?"

그가 영화사에서 계약금을 받았다고 덧붙이며 내게 돈뭉치를 쥐어주었다. 자신감의 원인이 그 돈뭉치 같았다. 나는 그 돈에서 숙박비를 제하고 소고기를 사왔다. 소고기를 굽는 동안 그들은 테라스에 앉아서 맥주를 들이키며 떠드느라 정신없었다. 인정할 건 인정해야겠다. 클린트 이스트우드는 타고난 배우였다. 나는 〈매디슨 카운티의 다리〉의 한 장면이라도 보는 듯 클린트 이스트우드와 여자가 이야기를 나누는 것을 넋을 놓고 바라봤다. 얼마 지나지 않아 여자가 잠시 화장실에 갔고 클린트 이스트우드는 휘청대며 내게 다가왔다.

"역시 최고의 안주는 여자야. 어때? 예쁘지 않나?"

그에게서 술 냄새가 풍겨왔다. 나는 긍정도 부정도 하지 않았다. 그는 자신이 사귄 여자들에 대해 이야기하기 시작했다. 정확히 기억나진 않지만 온갖 유명한 여배우들이 언급됐던 것 같다.

"자네 시나리오는 재미있긴 한데 말이지…… 뭔가 허전해."

absolutely miserable for waiting on a fading star like Clint Eastwood.

"Don't be too depressed, though. Everyone learns through their mistakes when they're young, you know? Would you by any chance want to work in Texas? I guarantee that you'll come up with something better there." He patted me on my shoulders.

"Anyway, wouldn't it be nice if we were in Texas? Nothing happens here. It's like nobody's living here. Thank God, I have beer, a woman, and steak now, though." He was annoying me by mentioning Texas, not knowing what I was feeling at that moment.

"All beef tastes the same! There's lots of American beef at E-Mart! If you swim in this reservoir, your mouth will fill with all kinds of beef!" I flew into a rage. In retrospect, it must have been my way of complaining to Clint Eastwood how even he couldn't understand my work. Surprised at my unusual outburst, he didn't seem to know what to say. At that moment, the woman returned, and Clint Eastwood backed out of the room, shooting sidelong glances at me as he left. He looked as if he had become used to the role of a coward.

As if they wanted to upset me more, Clint Eastwood and the woman made noise all night long.

그러던 중 그가 갑자기 진지한 표정을 짓더니 이렇게 말했다. 나는 그때서야 서랍에 든 시나리오를 그가 훔쳐봤다는 것을 깨달았다. 지금 생각해보면 그의 말은 일리가 있었다. 핑계 같지만 흉내만 냈을 뿐 내겐 인종 갈등과 베트남전처럼 명확한 상대가 없었다. 클린트 이스트우드가 할리우드에서 뛰쳐나온 것도 나와 같은 이유가 아니었을까, 라는 일종의 동질감도 느껴졌다. 그러나 그때 나는 감정적으로 달아올랐고 잠시나마 클린트 이스트우드를 그리워했던 게 말할 수 없이 후회됐으며 그와 같이 나도 이 세계에서 영원히 쇠퇴하는 기분이 들었다. 순간 맛이 간 클린트 이스트우드의 시중이나 들고 있는 내가 비참하게 느껴졌다.

"그렇다고 너무 의기소침해 있진 말게. 젊었을 땐 다 실수하면서 배우는 거 아니겠나. 혹시 텍사스에서 작업해볼 생각은 없나? 더 좋은 작품이 나올 거라 장담하네."

그가 이렇게 말하며 내 어깨를 두드렸다.

"그나저나 이곳이 텍사스였다면 더 좋았을 텐데 말이야. 여기는 아무 일도 일어나지 않아서 사람 사는 곳 같지 않단 말이지. 지금은 술과 여자와 스테이크가 있으

On an impulse, I decided to play *A Fistful of Dollars*. I probably hoped that Clint Eastwood would come into my office, look at his younger self, and feel embarrassed. But, nobody came into my office after midnight, and I couldn't enjoy the movie very well because of the woman's amorous moaning. I glared at the screen. An old man thirsting after a young hooker's body and the proud apostle of justice... Were they really the same person?

When Clint Eastwood in *A Fistful of Dollars* returned for vengeance to a remote Western village, someone knocked on the door of my office. When I opened the door, I found Clint Eastwood's woman standing there.

"Let's have a drink," she said, a smile in her eyes.

I asked her why she had come here. She should have been with Clint Eastwood. She said that he had fallen asleep, drunk out of his mind. Then she took a glance at the young Clint Eastwood on the screen. But she turned towards me almost immediately afterwards, as if she had lost interest in the movie.

"Looks like you were watching a movie. Am I bothering you?" she said. She didn't seem to even realize that the drunken old man sleeping next door and the young hero on the screen were the

니 그나마 다행이지만."

그는 상황 파악도 못 하고 예의 그 텍사스 타령을 하며 내 속을 긁어놓았다.

"소고기 맛은 다 똑같다고요. 시내 이마트에도 미국산 소고기가 널려 있어요. 이 저수지에서 헤엄만 쳐도 소 부속품들이 입 안에 가득 들어올걸요."

나는 화를 토해냈다. 돌이켜보면 그때 나는 클린트 이스트우드에게 당신마저 왜 내 작품을 이해해주지 못하느냐고 칭얼댔던 것 같다. 그는 평소와 다른 내 반응에 당황했는지 말을 잇지 못했다. 그때 여자가 돌아왔고 그는 내 눈치를 보며 뒤꽁무니를 뺐다. 아예 비겁한 도망자 역이 몸에 밴 것 같았다.

화를 돋우려 그러는지 그날 밤 내내 클린트 이스트우드와 여자는 소란을 피웠다. 나는 충동적으로 〈황야의 무법자〉를 틀었다. 클린트 이스트우드가 관리실에 들어와 자신의 젊은 시절을 보고 좌절했으면 하는 바람 때문이었던 것 같다. 그러나 자정이 지나도 관리실에는 아무도 들어오지 않았고 여자의 교성이 귓가에 맴돌아 영화를 제대로 감상할 수 없었다. 나는 화면을 노려봤다. 젊은 창녀의 육체를 탐하는 늙은이와 자존심을 지

same person. I said she wasn't, took a bottle of beer out of the fridge, and handed it to her.

"I heard you're a writer, is that right?" She sat next to me, her body touching mine, and drank a sip of beer.

I said that I hadn't made my literary debut yet and that I was just writing. It wasn't hard to guess what Clint Eastwood had said to her. He must have been busily making himself look better by belittling me. She insisted that I tell her what I was writing about.

"Nothing special. I don't think you'll find it interesting," I said. Still, she kept insisting and I began reluctantly to tell her about my work. Pretty soon, she turned to the TV, not paying attention to my story any longer. She must have been getting bored with my story. I stopped talking. There was nothing but silence for a while. Villains pointing guns were surrounding Clint Eastwood in the movie.

"Why do men like to fight so much?" she asked, turning away from the TV screen. I didn't know what to say. No wonder she couldn't understand my movie premise.

"By the way, is this guesthouse really that grandpa's?" she continued. I was too dumbstruck to respond. She seemed to interpret my silence as an

키는 정의의 사도…… 정녕 같은 인물이란 말인가.

〈황야의 무법자〉의 클린트 이스트우드가 복수를 하기 위해 서부의 외딴 마을에 되돌아왔을 무렵이었다. 누군가 관리실 문을 두드렸다. 문을 여니 클린트 이스트우드의 여자가 서 있었다.

"술 한잔해요."

그녀가 눈웃음을 치며 말했다. 나는 클린트 이스트우드는 어떻게 하고 여기에 왔냐고 물었다. 그녀는 그가 술에 취해 곯아떨어졌다고 말한 뒤 화면 속 젊은 클린트 이스트우드를 흘끗 봤다. 그리고 금세 흥미를 잃었는지 내 쪽으로 다시 고개를 돌렸다.

"영화 보고 있었나 봐요. 방해한 건 아니죠?"

그녀가 말했다. 옆방에서 곯아떨어진 노인과 같은 사람인지 짐작조차 못하는 모양이었다. 나는 괜찮다고 말한 뒤 냉장고에서 맥주를 꺼내 그녀에게 건넸다.

"작가라면서요?"

그녀가 내 옆에 바싹 붙어 앉아 맥주를 한 모금 마셨다. 나는 정식 작가는 아니며 습작을 하고 있을 뿐이라고 말했다. 클린트 이스트우드가 어떤 말을 했는지 뻔했다. 나를 짓이겨서 자신의 우월함을 뽐내느라 정신없

affirmative answer.

"Who is that grandpa, anyways?" she asked, and took another sip of her beer.

"Clint Eastwood," I said. She shrugged, as if to say that she had no idea who that was.

"He's a famous actor."

"A movie actor?" she asked. I nodded over to the TV screen. Young and handsome, Clint Eastwood was firing shots at a villain at that very moment. She looked at me doubtfully.

"Is he as famous as Woody Allen?" she asked and then began talking about *You Will Meet a Tall Dark Stranger*, which she had just seen a while ago. In my opinion, *You Will Meet a Tall Dark Stranger* just belittled its audience by packaging a trifling story with a spurious message. Anybody who saw her talking about things that were inessential to the core of the movie—the film score, or Anthony Hopkins' cuteness, etc.—could guess how ridiculous that movie was. I was thinking of Clint Eastwood's lonely bed, while pretending to agree with her.

"How could someone as strong as that not last three minutes?" Her rambling that had begun with *You Will Meet a Tall Dark Stranger* had arrived at a comparison between the young Clint Eastwood on

었겠지. 그녀는 내게 무엇을 쓰고 있는지 말해달라고 졸랐다.

"빤한 이야기죠, 뭐. 재미없을 거예요."

내가 답했다. 그래도 그녀는 계속 졸랐고 나는 못 이기는 척 이야기하기 시작했다. 얼마 지나지 않아 그녀는 내 얘기를 듣는 둥 마는 둥 하며 화면으로 눈을 돌렸다. 내 시나리오가 지루한 모양이었다. 나는 얘기를 멈췄다. 한동안 침묵이 이어졌다. 화면 속 클린트 이스트우드 주위로 총을 든 악당들이 몰려들고 있었다.

"남자들은 대체 왜 저렇게 싸우는 걸 좋아하죠?"

여자가 화면에서 눈길을 떼며 물었다. 말문이 막혔다. 내 시나리오를 이해하지 못하는 게 당연했다.

"근데 이 펜션 진짜 저 할아버지 소유예요?"

여자가 이어서 물었다. 나는 기가 차서 아무 말도 하지 못했다. 여자는 그런 내 행동을 긍정의 의미로 받아들이는 듯했다.

"저 할아버지가 누군데요?"

그녀가 맥주를 들이키며 물었다.

"클린트 이스트우드."

내가 답했다. 그녀는 모르겠다는 듯 어깨를 으쓱했다.

the screen and the current Clint Eastwood. She was griping about him, saying that she had almost vomited because of his foul breath and creepy black spots. It was around then that Clint Eastwood returned. He frowned and asked her what she was doing here.

"I've done what I was paid to do, right?" she retorted, arguing that it was none of his business; she had worked as much as she'd been paid for. Clint Eastwood took several long steps towards her, and then slapped her across her face.

"Act your age!" she shouted back at him.

Clint Eastwood took his gun out and aimed it at her. The woman began trembling and whimpering. While the Clint Eastwood on the screen punished an outlaw in the name of justice, the real Clint Eastwood was threatening a woman with an empty gun for the sake of his pathetic pride. Thinking that the scene in front of me was funnier than any movie, I waited for the climax.

Uncle died. I returned home after his funeral to find that Clint Eastwood had disappeared. My office lock had been broken and some of my money had disappeared. There was a note on the desk. He wrote that he regretted for not talking to me more

"유명한 영화배우예요."

"영화배우요?"

그녀가 반문했다. 나는 텔레비전을 향해 고갯짓했다. 그녀는 화면으로 눈을 돌렸다. 화면 속에서는 젊고 잘생긴 클린트 이스트우드가 악당을 향해 총을 쏘고 있었다. 그녀는 의혹이 가득한 눈으로 다시 나를 봤다.

"우디 앨런만큼 유명한가요?"

그녀는 이렇게 물은 뒤 얼마 전에 극장에서 본 〈환상의 그대〉에 대해 떠벌리기 시작했다. 내가 볼 때 〈환상의 그대〉는 볼품없는 이야기에 그럴듯한 의미를 부여해서 관객을 우롱하는 영화에 불과했다. 그녀가 영화음악이 너무 좋았다는 둥, 안소니 홉킨스가 너무 귀엽다는 둥, 영화와 전혀 관계없는 말만 늘어놓고 있는 걸 보면 〈환상의 그대〉가 얼마나 대책 없는 영화인지 누구나 짐작할 수 있을 것이다. 그때 나는 아마 그녀의 말에 동의하는 척하며 외롭게 잠든 클린트 이스트우드를 떠올리고 있었던 것 같다.

"저렇게 강인한 사람이 지금은 어떻게 삼 분을 못 버텨요?"

〈환상의 그대〉에서 시작한 수다는 어느새 화면 속 클

about my pitch, and then went ahead and discussed its strengths and weaknesses. A few of the comments were good pieces of advice, but most of them were nonsensical. Then, he wrote that he had to leave for urgent business without saying good-bye and that he was borrowing some money from me. Also, he wrote that he would find me a good place where I could concentrate on my creative writing in Texas and that he would treat me with fresh milk and steak, if I ever decided to visit Texas. He ended his note by saying that he would be at the pub called "Old Texas" near the city hall of Austin every night, so I should come look for him there whenever I wanted.

Two days later, a person from a movie production company showed up at my guesthouse, looking for Clint Eastwood. I told him that Clint Eastwood had disappeared. Then he asked me where he had gone and I said I didn't know. He said he would take legal measures. I told him he should do whatever he liked. A few days later, a young detective came to the guesthouse. He was also looking for Clint Eastwood. He said that someone had accused Clint Eastwood of having committed assault and battery. It must have been that hooker. Knowing that Clint Eastwood was an actor, she

린트 이스트우드와 실제 클린트 이스트우드를 비교하는 데까지 이르렀다. 그녀는 클린트 이스트우드의 구취가 구역질 난다느니, 온몸에 핀 검버섯이 징그럽다느니 호들갑을 떨기 시작했다. 클린트 이스트우드가 관리실에 들어온 건 그 무렵이었다. 그는 인상을 쓰며 여자에게 왜 여기 있느냐고 물었다.

"내가 할 일은 끝났는데요?"

여자는 지지 않고 돈을 받은 만큼 일했는데 무슨 상관이냐고 덤볐다. 클린트 이스트우드는 이쪽으로 성큼성큼 다가와 여자의 빰을 때렸다.

"나잇값을 해야지."

여자가 악을 썼다. 그러자 클린트 이스트우드가 허리춤에 찬 총을 여자에게 겨누었다. 여자는 소리를 지르며 벌벌 떨기 시작했다. 화면 속 클린트 이스트우드는 정의를 위해 악당을 벌하고 있었고, 현실의 클린트 이스트우드는 알량한 자존심을 위해 빈총으로 여자를 위협하고 있었다. 나는 그 어떤 영화보다도 눈앞에서 벌어지는 상황이 재미있다고 생각하며 극의 클라이맥스를 기다리고 있었다.

must have decided to make the most of the situation and make some more money. I told the detective that Clint Eastwood was gone. The detective had heard the perpetrator was a famous film star and he asked me who he was.

"Clint Eastwood," I said.

The detective did not seem to know who that was. Suddenly, I felt upset. I felt like yelling, "He may be old now, but he used to be much stronger than you ever could be!"

"She must have been mistaken. He's not a film star, but an American traveler," I said despite my urge to start yelling. I didn't feel like bothering about any explanations, especially when there was no way the detective would understand. The detective slowly nodded his head.

Soon afterwards, I sold the guesthouse Uncle had bequeathed me and left for Texas. It wasn't to meet Clint Eastwood. I was exhausted after my uncle's funeral and my writing had not been going very well. Besides, I had some money, so I wanted to enjoy a vacation. I chose Texas because I hoped that my writing would go well in the home of the Western, as Clint Eastwood had claimed.

After I arrived in Texas, I toured the area for a few days. The first place I visited was the Alamo,

숙부가 죽었다. 장례를 치르고 와보니 클린트 이스트우드는 사라지고 없었다. 관리실의 자물쇠는 부서져 있었고 얼마간의 돈도 사라진 상태였다. 책상 위에는 쪽지가 하나 남아 있었다. 클린트 이스트우드는 쪽지에 지난번에는 얼마 말하지 못해 아쉬웠다며 내 시나리오의 장단점을 꼽아놓았다. 몇 마디는 새겨들을 만했지만 대부분 헛소리였다. 그다음에는 급한 일이 생겨 인사도 못 하고 떠나게 됐다면서 돈을 조금만 꿔가겠다는 내용이 적혀 있었다. 또 텍사스를 방문하면 창작에 몰두할 만한 작업실을 알아봐줄 뿐만 아니라 신선한 우유와 스테이크를 대접하겠다고 덧붙여 쓰여 있었다. 마지막으로 그는 매일 밤 어스틴 시청 부근에 있는 '올드 텍사스'란 펍에 있을 테니 언제든지 와서 자신을 찾으라고 말했다.

그로부터 이틀 뒤였다. 영화사 관계자가 펜션에 왔다. 그는 클린트 이스트우드를 찾았다. 나는 클린트 이스트우드가 사라졌다고 말했다. 그는 클린트 이스트우드의 행방을 물었고 나는 모른다고 말했다. 그는 법적인 조치를 취한다고 했다. 나는 좋을 대로 하라고 답했다. 며칠 뒤에는 젊은 형사가 찾아왔다. 그는 폭행죄로 고소

the fierce battleground of the American War of Independence. Although I found old men wearing the American War of Independence era military outfits interesting at first, I lost my interest after taking a couple of pictures. They were as lifeless as stuffed animals in a museum. The next day, I went to the Rio Grande. The Rio Grande was crowded with tourists who had come to enjoy rafting and souvenir-selling mestizos. It was as crowded as a shopping mall and so, without really enjoying the scenery, I returned to my hotel as if I was fleeing someone's company. The next day, I went to the desert near a tourist ranch in San Antonio. There were so many buildings there in that desert that, in comparison to the buildings, there seemed to be only a handful of sand. A film crew was working full steam ahead in a corner of the desert. The guide explained that they were filming a Western. I couldn't really see actors. Only their enormous cameras and instruments were visible. I saw that movie later in Korea, but the movie was more like a rebellion against the Western than the Western itself. A young girl was its main character.

I no longer felt inclined to go on a tour. So I found a place to stay near the Rio Grande and began to concentrate on my writing. It was not a

가 들어왔다며 클린트 이스트우드를 찾았다. 그 여자가 클린트 이스트우드를 신고한 모양이었다. 영화배우라는 말을 듣고 단단히 한몫 잡기로 한 것 같았다. 나는 지금 클린트 이스트우드가 없다고 답했다. 형사는 가해자가 유명한 영화배우라는 말을 들었다면서 그가 누구인지 설명해달라고 했다.

"클린트 이스트우드요."

내가 말했다. 형사는 말을 못 알아듣는 눈치였다. 나는 갑자기 열이 받았다. 지금은 늙었지만 예전엔 당신보다 훨씬 힘이 셌다고요. 나는 이렇게 퍼붓고 싶었다.

"착각한 모양이네요. 영화배우가 아니라 그냥 미국에서 온 여행객이었어요."

속마음과는 달리 나는 그냥 이렇게 덧붙였다. 일일이 설명하기 귀찮았고 알아들을 리도 없었기 때문이었다. 그때서야 형사는 고개를 천천히 끄덕였다.

얼마 지나지 않아 나는 숙부가 유산으로 남긴 펜션을 처분한 뒤 텍사스로 떠났다. 클린트 이스트우드를 만나기 위해서는 아니었다. 장례를 치르느라 지쳤고 시나리오도 풀리지 않았으며 유산도 생긴 터라 휴가를 보내고 올 생각이었다. 텍사스를 택한 건 무엇보다 서부극의

place, though, where I had a full view of the Rio Grande. I couldn't find a spot like that. Well, I could catch a glimpse of the Rio Grande from my hotel room for sure, but I wasn't getting any inspiration because of the noise and light swarming the area. Besides, it was really humid and damp, probably because of its location near the river. I could write better at my uncle's guesthouse. In the end, I moved to a small hotel near the city hall.

From then on, I began to wander around the area in search of "Old Texas." Perhaps, I wanted to meet Clint Eastwood and tell him that I couldn't even write well in Texas, either. Or, perhaps, I was just lonely. I can't remember. It was too long ago. But I can clearly remember that the "Old Texas" Clint Eastwood had mentioned was nowhere to be found. Downtown was full of hotels and casinos. I wondered if Clint Eastwood had tricked me again.

The vast desert was covered with concrete, the native Texans were infinitely kind, and the police officers were excessively concerned about the safety of tourists. Instead of cows, cars went back and forth in an orderly manner. Even prostitution was legal so the customers didn't feel guilty as long as they had money. Unlike Clint Eastwood's depictions, Texas was boring, an almost cruelly com-

본고장에 가면 클린트 이스트우드의 말대로 시나리오가 잘 풀릴 거란 일말의 기대가 있었기 때문이었다.

텍사스에 도착한 뒤 며칠간은 관광을 했다. 첫 행선지는 독립전쟁의 격전지 알라모였다. 독립전쟁 당시 군복을 입은 노인들이 이목을 끌었지만 박물관에 전시된 박제처럼 생동감이 없어서 사진을 한두 번 찍으니 금세 흥미가 떨어졌다. 이튿날에는 리오그란데에 다녀왔다. 리오그란데에는 급류타기를 하러 온 관광객들과 특산품을 팔고 있는 메스티소 인디언들이 들끓었다. 쇼핑몰을 방불케 할 만큼 복잡하기 그지없어서 나는 리오그란데의 풍경도 제대로 보지 못하고 쫓기듯 숙소로 돌아왔다. 다음 날에는 샌안토니오 관광 목장 근처 사막에 갔다. 사막에는 수많은 건물들이 촘촘히 박혀 있었는데, 그에 비하면 모래는 한 줌도 안 돼 보였다. 사막 한쪽에서는 영화 촬영이 한창이었다. 가이드는 서부극을 촬영하는 중이라고 설명했다. 그러나 거대한 카메라와 장비들만 보일 뿐 배우들은 보이지 않았다. 나중에 한국에서 그 영화를 봤지만 이건 거의 서부극에 대한 반란이었다. 어린 여자아이가 주인공이었던 것이다.

나는 그때부터 관광할 기분이 나지 않아 리오그란데

fortable space like my uncle's guesthouse. The Texas of my imagination was a lawless place; it needed justice and a hero. But present day Texas didn't need a hero. There was no trace of a Texas I knew.

While I wandering around feeling depressed, I bumped into another passerby. He gave me a dirty look. He looked as threatening as Lee Marvin in *Point Blank*. Scared, I instinctively apologized profusely, backing away as I did. Perhaps realizing that I was a tourist, he immediately smiled awkwardly and asked me if I'd been hurt. He seemed to be well aware of the fact that I was there to spend money.

"What are you looking for? May I help you?" he asked me gently. But he must not have actually meant to help me. When I was about to ask him where "Old Texas" was, Lee Marvin turned around and disappeared into the crowd. I wandered around some more and then ate a steak at a restaurant among the crowd of tourists. Although there were advertisements for Texas beef here and there, the steak tasted about the same as the steak in Korea.

About a fortnight after I arrived in Texas, I entered my hotel after wandering around the streets,

근방에 숙소를 잡고 본격적으로 시나리오를 쓰기 시작했다. 그러나 클린트 이스트우드의 말처럼 리오그란데가 내다보이는 숙소는 찾을 수 없었다. 아니, 리오그란데가 언뜻 보이긴 했지만 소란과 불빛이 들끓어서 영감에 귀를 기울일 수 없었다. 더군다나 강 옆이라 그런지 습도가 높아 축축하고 끕끕했다. 펜션보다 글이 더 안 써지는 것 같았다. 나는 결국 리오그란데를 벗어나 시청 근처의 작은 호텔에 자리를 잡았다.

그 이후 나는 밤마다 '올드 텍사스'를 찾아 헤매기 시작했다. 클린트 이스트우드에게 텍사스에서도 글이 안 써지는 건 마찬가지라고 따져 묻고 싶었던 건지 단지 외로워서 그랬던 건지는 오랜 시간이 흘렀기 때문에 잘 모르겠다. 다만 '올드 텍사스'가 어디에도 없었다는 건 확실히 기억난다. 클린트 이스트우드가 나를 또 기만한 게 아닐까, 라는 생각이 들 만큼 시내에는 온통 호텔과 카지노와 클럽뿐이었다. 광활한 사막은 콘크리트로 메워진 상태였고 현지인들은 한없이 친절했으며 경찰들은 관광객들의 안전을 챙기느라 과도한 신경을 쓰고 있었다. 소 떼 대신 차들이 질서정연하게 차도를 오갔고 매춘도 합법이어서 돈만 있으면 죄책감을 느낄 필요도

having spent hours looking for "Old Texas" in vain. There was a strange old man sitting in the lobby with a newspaper in front of him. Seeing me enter, he winked at me and greeted me. He seemed to be saying, "Welcome to Texas!" He asked me where I was from, smiling at me interestedly. I said I'd come from Korea and walked over to him.

"Do *you* know anything about 'Old Texas'?" I asked him.

He answered that he did. He described it vividly. And he said that although he had moved to California to live with his daughter, he'd used to hang out at "Old Texas" with his office mates. He also said that he was visiting Texas because his friend had died. He added that "Old Texas," a small pub in the old days, was renovated and had become a club called "Blue Sea." I remembered seeing it—a giant, neon-lit club—two blocks away from the city hall. I thanked him and went out again.

"This place is hell now," he said as I left.

When I entered "Blue Sea," I was confronted with loud music and drunken people of various ethnicities swaying and rocking to the music. I looked around, but I couldn't find any lonely old, expressionless men drinking rum, let alone Clint East-

없었다. 클린트 이스트우드의 말과 달리 텍사스도 숙부의 펜션만큼이나 심심하고 잔인하리만치 쾌적한 공간이었다. 내 상상의 텍사스는 무법의 공간이었기 때문에 정의와 영웅이 필요했다. 그러나 이제 텍사스에 영웅은 필요 없었다. 내가 아는 텍사스는 없었다.

침울한 심경에 잠겨 거리를 배회하던 중이었다. 행인과 어깨를 부딪쳤다. 그는 나를 꼬나봤다. 〈포인트 블랭크〉의 리 마빈처럼 험상궂게 생긴 남자였다. 나는 나도 모르게 겁이 나 연신 사과를 하며 뒷걸음질을 쳤다. 그는 내가 관광객이라는 걸 알아챘는지 이내 부자연스러운 웃음을 지으며 어디 다친 데는 없냐고 말을 걸었다. 내가 자신의 돈줄이라는 걸 아주 잘 알고 있는 듯했다.

"어디 찾으시나요? 도와드릴까요?"

그가 상냥하게 물었다. 그러나 그마저도 빈말인 듯 내가 '올드 텍사스'에 대해 물으려는 사이 리 마빈은 등을 돌려 사라져버렸다. 나는 다시 거리를 배회하다가 관광객 무리에 휩싸여 레스토랑에서 스테이크를 먹었다. 텍사스 산 소고기를 치켜세우는 광고가 여기저기 붙어 있었지만 한국에서 먹는 것과 별 차이는 없었다.

텍사스에 온 지 보름이 지나서였다. 그날도 나는 '올

wood. Actually, to be more accurate, there wasn't any room for that kind of a man in that noisy space. All of a sudden, I began to feel that all these people of diverse ethnicities mixing with one another under these gaudy lights seemed excessively artificial. I missed the Western honesty of in-your-face antagonism and constant fighting, the dust-covered men exhausted from their fights on their way home. Feeling extremely tired for no reason, I sat down at the bar and ordered a beer.

"What brings you to Texas?" the bartender asked, handing me a beer. He was a young man with a sturdy build in his late-twenties. He was wearing a cowboy outfit, but kept adjusting it. It looked as if he was uncomfortable in it. I somehow felt as if he was the epitome of all Texan young men who hated the name Clint Eastwood.

"I came to look for someone," I said. The bartender said he could help me and asked who I was looking for.

"Clint Eastwood."

"Who?" he asked me again, probably unable to hear because of the loud music.

"Clint Eastwood," I said again, this time into his ear.

Fortunately, he knew Clint Eastwood. He said his

드 텍사스'를 찾아 헤맸다가 허탕을 치고 호텔에 들어섰다. 로비에는 낯선 노신사가 신문을 펼친 채 앉아 있었다. 그는 내가 들어가자 눈을 찡긋하며 인사했다. "텍사스에 온 걸 환영하오"라고 말하는 듯했다. 그는 내게 어디에서 왔냐고 물으며 관심을 표했다. 나는 한국에서 왔다고 답한 뒤 그에게 다가갔다.

"올드 텍사스를 아십니까?"

내가 물었다. 노인은 '올드 텍사스'를 안다고 답했다. 그는 '올드 텍사스'를 생생하게 묘사했는데, 지금은 그가 딸과 함께 살기 위해 캘리포니아로 이사했고 예전에 직장 동료들과 어울려 '올드 텍사스'에 자주 드나들었으며 친구가 죽는 바람에 오랜만에 텍사스에 왔다는 이야기밖에 기억나지 않는다. 그는 이어서 '올드 텍사스'가 예전에는 자그마한 펍이었는데 오랜만에 텍사스에 와 보니 '블루 씨'라는 클럽으로 재건축됐다고 말했다. '블루 씨'는 시청에서 두 블록 거리에 있는 거대한 클럽으로 나도 몇 번이나 지나친 적이 있었다. 나는 그에게 감사를 표한 뒤 밖으로 나섰다.

"이곳은 이제 지옥이라오."

노인의 목소리가 등 뒤에서 들렸다.

grandmother was a Clint Eastwood fan. He then added that he had seen his movies a few times with his grandmother when he was young, but that he could no longer remember them.

"I heard that this used to be his hangout," I said.

Raising an eyebrow, the bartender said that the "Blue Sea" had recently reopened with a new owner and that he hadn't worked here long. He also added that, as far as he knew, Clint Eastwood had disappeared from Texas long ago, and since his grandparents had died.

I talked about this and that with that bartender a little longer. I believe I drank quite a bit, watching the club scenes when we had nothing more to talk about. A beautiful dark-skinned woman who resembled Penelope Cruz sat down next to me around then. She seemed interested in me, asking where I was from. We talked about movies for a while. Since we didn't talk about Woody Allen, she must have been someone whom I could have had a decent conversation with.

Suddenly, someone touched my shoulder. I turned around to find a solidly built black man standing right in front of me. Frowning, he grabbed Penelope Cruz and threw her down on the floor. He swore at her and advanced towards me.

'블루 씨'에 들어서자 전자음악이 시끄럽게 울려 퍼지는 가운데 여러 인종들이 술에 취해 몸을 흐느적거리는 게 보였다. 주위를 살폈지만 클린트 이스트우드는커녕 무표정한 얼굴로 럼주를 마시는 고독한 남자 하나 눈에 띄지 않았다. 이 소란스러운 공간에는 그런 남자가 있을 틈이 없다고 하는 게 좀더 정확한 표현일 것이다. 불현듯 현란한 조명 아래 뒤섞인 다양한 인종들이 더할 나위 없이 인위적으로 느껴지기 시작했다. 서로에 대한 절대적인 증오를 드러내고 싸움을 일삼는 서부의 솔직함과 기나긴 전투에 지친 채 다리를 끌고 귀가하는 먼지투성이의 남자들이 그리워졌다. 나는 왠지 모를 피로를 느끼며 바에 앉아 맥주를 주문했다.

"텍사스엔 웬일이에요?"

바텐더가 맥주를 내놓으며 말을 붙였다. 이십대 후반 정도로 보이는 골격이 큰 젊은이였다. 그는 카우보이 복장 차림이었는데, 옷이 불편한지 자꾸 옷매무새를 매만지고 있었다. 나는 왠지 그가 클린트 이스트우드라는 이름을 증오하는 텍사스의 젊은이들을 상징하는 것처럼 느껴졌다.

"The hell is this? Some little punk like you touching my woman? Listen, why don't you walk away and go back to your country while you're at it!" he barked, thrusting his face into mine. A crowd began to gather around us. They began to jeer like we were in a scene from *Cool Hand Luke*. Although I should have been scared, I was almost happy with the situation. It felt like I was in an introduction to a movie that I had always wanted to see. Wasn't it the movie scenario that I had always wanted, a conflict breaking out over a beautiful woman, a hero suddenly appearing to punish the villain?

"Texas may not be a place for me, for sure. But it also sure as hell isn't a place for you, either!" I answered. The man took me by the collar and hauled me up. I was unfazed and stood my ground. We yelled at each other for a while. He raised his fist abruptly. The crowd was cheering. I closed my eyes tight. But, suddenly, it became completely quiet. I opened my eyes slowly. Somebody was pointing a gun at the man's temple.

"Hey, kid! Let's just relax here! He's my friend," the newcomer said in a raspy voice. It was Clint Eastwood. I still remember the tired look on his face, as if he'd arrived there after a long, heroic chase after some villain. He put his finger in the

"사람을 찾으러 왔습니다."

내가 말했다. 바텐더는 알아봐준다며 찾는 이가 누구냐고 물었다.

"클린트 이스트우드요."

"뭐라고요?"

바텐더가 음악이 너무 커서 내 목소리가 잘 들리지 않는 듯 바짝 다가와 재차 물었다.

"클린트 이스트우드라고요."

나는 바텐더의 귀에 대고 말했다. 다행히 바텐더는 클린트 이스트우드를 알고 있었다. 바텐더는 자신의 할머니가 클린트 이스트우드의 팬이라고 말했다. 그리고 어렸을 때 할머니를 따라 몇 번 클린트 이스트우드의 영화를 본 적이 있는데 지금은 기억나지 않는다고 했다.

"여기 단골이라고 들었어요."

내가 말했다. 바텐더는 고개를 갸우뚱하면서 '블루 씨'가 얼마 전 주인이 바뀐 데다 새로 개장했고 자신은 여기서 일한 지 얼마 되지 않는다고 말했다. 또 자신이 알기로는 클린트 이스트우드가 텍사스에서 자취를 감춘 건 자신의 조부모가 죽은 것만큼이나 한참 됐다고 덧붙였다.

gun's trigger guard, and then gave me a big smile.

"How about that! This is Texas," his smile seemed to say.

Translated by Jeon Seung-hee

그 뒤로 바텐더와 시시콜콜한 이야기를 몇 마디 더 나누었던 것 같다. 얘깃거리가 떨어질 때쯤엔 클럽의 풍경을 구경하며 술을 마셨던 것 같다. 페넬로페 크루즈를 닮은 까무잡잡하고 아름다운 여자가 내 옆에 앉은 건 그 무렵이었다. 그녀는 내게 어느 나라에서 왔냐고 물으며 관심을 보였다. 그 뒤 우리는 영화에 대해 꽤 오랫동안 이야기를 나눴다. 우디 앨런 얘기는 나오지 않았으니 적어도 대화가 통화는 상대였던 건 분명하다. 그때였다. 누군가 내 어깨를 두드렸다. 돌아보니 기골이 장대한 흑인이 서 있었다. 그는 얼굴을 일그러뜨리곤 페넬로페 크루즈를 낚아채 바닥에 쓰러뜨렸다. 그리고 그녀에게 욕설을 내뱉은 뒤 내게 다가왔다.

"너 같은 놈이 내 여자를 건들다니 치욕스럽군. 네 나라로 당장 돌아가."

그가 내게 얼굴을 드밀며 말했다. 그때 한 무리의 사람들이 몰려들어 우리를 에워싸기 시작했다. 그들은 〈폭력탈옥〉의 한 장면처럼 내게 야유를 퍼부었다. 겁을 먹어야 마땅했지만 당시 나는 왠지 이 상황이 내가 그토록 갈망하던 영화의 도입부처럼 느껴져 반가울 지경이었다. 아름다운 여자로 인해 갈등이 생기고 영웅이 나타나 악인을 처단하는 게 내가 원하던 시나리오 아닌가.

"텍사스는 내가 있을 곳도 아니지만 흑인이 설치는 곳도 아니지."

내가 대꾸했다. 흑인이 내 멱살을 잡고 자리에서 일으켰다. 나도 지지 않고 그에게 덤벼들었다. 우리는 얼마간 설전을 벌였다. 그러던 중 그가 주먹을 치켜들었다. 주위를 둘러싼 사람들이 환호성을 질렀다. 나는 눈을 질끈 감았다. 그러나 이상하게도 별안간 사위가 고요해졌다. 나는 눈을 슬며시 떴다. 누군가 흑인의 관자놀이에 총을 겨누고 있었다.

"이봐, 애송이. 그 손 놓게. 내 친구라네."

가래 섞인 목소리, 클린트 이스트우드였다. 나는 아직도 기억한다. 악당과 기나긴 추격전을 마치고 온 듯한 클린트 이스트우드의 고단한 표정을. 클린트 이스트우드는 방아쇠에 손가락을 건 뒤 나를 보고 활짝 웃었다. "어때? 여기가 텍사스야"라고 말하는 듯했다.

창작노트
Writer's Note

1

「나의 클린트 이스트우드」는 클린트 이스트우드에 대한 소설이다. 우리가 익히 알고 있는 감독 겸 배우 클린트 이스트우드 말이다. 내가 클린트 이스트우드를 택한 건 다른 이유가 있어서가 아니라 클린트 이스트우드를 좋아하기 때문이다. 나는 클린트 이스트우드를 동경한다. 공화당원인 클린트 이스트우드 때문에 좌파를 자처하는 친구와 다투기도 했다.

나는 클린트 이스트우드를 공화당원과 감독이 아닌 배우로서 좋아한다. 그가 만든 작품들은 작품성이 있을지는 모르겠지만 내겐 그리 매력 있는 작품들이 아니었

1

"My Clint Eastwood" is a story about Clint Eastwood—the Clint Eastwood we all know well as director and actor. I chose to write about him because I like him. I long for him. I even quarreled with a liberal friend over Clint Eastwood, a noted Republican.

I like Clint Eastwood not as a Republican or as a director, but as an actor. The movies he's directed may be fairly artistic, but they aren't very attractive to me. The Clint Eastwood I like is not the intellectual, professional Eastwood, pitching movies, directing, and supporting political parties. Although I can't say why exactly, I'm not interested in Clint

다. 그러니까 내가 좋아하는 클린트 이스트우드는 이성을 지닌(시나리오를 쓰고 촬영 현장을 지위하며 정당을 지지하는) 클린트 이스트우드가 아니다. 구체적인 이유는 짐작할 수 없지만 나는 사유하는 클린트 이스트우드에게 별 관심이 없다.

위와 같은 생각을 품기 시작한 건 돈 시겔의 〈일망타진〉을 본 뒤였다. 솔직히 말해 영화는 정확히 기억나지 않는다. 영화를 일부러 다시 볼 생각도 없다. (소설을 반복해 보는 것과 달리 나는 한 번 본 영화를 다시 보지 않는다) 〈일망타진〉을 생각하면 어렴풋이 범죄자를 쫓는 보안관 클린트 이스트우드가 떠오른다. 아름다운 여자에게 강제로 키스하는 클린트 이스트우드가 떠오른다. 유럽의 배우가 갖지 못하는 어떤 단호함이 클린트 이스트우드에게 엿보인다. 그는 젊음, 강인한 육체, 본능의 상징이다. 어쩌면 내가 젊은 배우 클린트 이스트우드를 좋아하는 건 그의 남성성 때문일지도 모른다. 나는 가끔 내가 코맥 매카시의 『로드』의 아이라면 아무런 고민 없이 클린트 이스트우드를 따라 나설 것이라고 생각한다.

Eastwood as a thinking person.

I began to develop an interest in Clint Eastwood as an actor after I watched Don Siegel's *Coogan's Bluff*. Honestly, I don't remember the details of the movie very well anymore. I don't have any intention to watch it again. (Although I often re-read novels, I don't watch movies repeatedly). When I think of *Coogan's Bluff*, I can vaguely remember the young deputy sheriff Clint Eastwood. I also remember him forcing a kiss on a woman. I could see certain resoluteness in Clint Eastwood, a quality European actors didn't seem to have. He was a symbol of youth, toughness, and instinct. I like Clint Eastwood as a young actor perhaps because of this masculinity. I sometimes think that if I were the child in Cormack McCarthy's *The Road*, I would follow Clint Eastwood without thinking twice.

2

I originally did not mean to write a story about Clint Eastwood. Clint Eastwood is a real person living in a real world. As a fan of his, I was afraid of delving into the mysteries and secrets of his life. It seemed like a burden.

The original title to "My Clint Eastwood" was "Unforgiven." But, the closer the story came to its

2

처음부터 클린트 이스트우드에 대한 소설을 쓰고 싶었던 건 아니다. 아무래도 그는 현실에 존재하는 사람이었다. 클린트 이스트우드를 좋아하는 만큼 나는 그의 인생에 손을 대기 겁났고 부담스러웠다.

「나의 클린트 이스트우드」의 원래 제목은 '용서받지 못한 자'였다. 그러나 소설이 완성돼 갈수록 이 소설이 클린트 이스트우드의 실제 삶과는 다르다는 생각이 들었다. 그러자 거짓말을 하고 있다는 죄책감이 들었다. 스트레스를 많이 받았다. 그 이후 나는 '나의 클린트 이스트우드'로 제목을 바꿨다. 좀 더 수월하게 소설을 써나갈 수 있었다.

아무튼 나는 「나의 클린트 이스트우드」를 쓰기 직전 자연사 박물관에서 일하는 중년 남자 W에 대한 소설을 쓰고 있었다. 정확한 내용은 기억나지 않는데, W는 어떤 이유로 화자의 추적을 당하고 있다. 화자는 W의 집 근처에 있는 카페에 앉아 W의 행적을 기록했다. 그 카페에는 〈용서받지 못한 자〉의 포스터가 걸려 있다. 그 포스터 속 클린트 이스트우드에 대해 나는 다음과 같이 설명했다.

completion, the more clearly I realized that this story was quite different from Clint Eastwood's real life. Then, I began feeling guilty for telling falsehoods about him. I was stressed. After I changed the title to "My Clint Eastwood" I was able to finish the story much easier.

At any rate, before I began to write "My Clint Eastwood," I was writing a story about W, a middle-aged man working in a natural history museum. I cannot remember the details, but the narrator was chasing W for some reason. The narrator sits in a café near W's house and records W's every movement. A poster for the movie *Unforgiven* hangs on one of the cafe's walls. I described the Clint Eastwood on that poster in this way:

Clint Eastwood is old now. These days, people rarely know that he was once an actor before he was a director. Young women, especially, don't have any memories of his former tough guy past behind his now frail, old body. They know him only as an old, hard-grained director. His change in appearance is probably a matter of hormones. Men lose their voice and hair after they become middle aged. Alain Delon, Micky Rourke, Al Pacino, Robert De Niro... All they can do these days is to

'클린트 이스트우드는 이제 늙었다. 그가 감독이기 이전에 배우였다는 사실을 아는 이는 드물다. 특히 젊은 여자들은 그의 쇠약한 육체와 과거의 강인함을 함께 떠올리지 못한다. 그저 깐깐해 보이는 노감독 정도로 기억할 뿐이다. 어쩌면 호르몬의 문제일지도 모른다. 중년이 지나 목소리와 머리칼이 얇아지고 있는 남자들…… 알랭 들롱, 미키 루크, 알 파치노, 로버트 드 니로…… 지금 그들이 할 수 있는 거라곤 쇠락한 옛 명성을 보전하기 위해 시시껄렁한 조연을 맡아 고군분투하는 것뿐이다.'

그렇다. 「나의 클린트 이스트우드」에도 같은 문장들이 들어간다. 나는 어느 순간부터 W에 대한 소설이 아니라 「나의 클린트 이스트우드」를 쓰고 있었다.

3

「나의 클린트 이스트우드」는 인물에 대한 소설이다. 인물에 대한 소설을 쓴 건 처음이다. 로베르토 볼라뇨의 영향인 거 같다. 볼라뇨의 단편집 『전화』에는 인물에 대한 소설이 주를 이룬다. 「엔리케 마르틴」「센시니」「앤 무어의 삶」「굼벵이 아저씨」…… 내가 볼라뇨의 단편들

take on trivial supporting roles and work hard to live up to their withering legacy.

These same sentences appear in "My Clint Eastwood." At some point while writing a story about W, I was writing "My Clint Eastwood."

3

"My Clint Eastwood" is a story about a single character. This is my first attempt at writing a story about a character. Roberto Bolano might have influenced me. His collection of short stories, *Phone Calls*, mainly feature stories centered around a single character—"Enrique Martin," "Sensini," "Anne Moore's Life," and "The Grub," to name a few. I believe "My Clint Eastwood" presents what I felt reading Bolano's stories and the influence they had on me.

4

I sometimes imagine Clint Eastwood reading "My Clint Eastwood" and chuckling. He might say, "Hey, pal! Welcome to my life!"

에서 어떤 영향을 받았고 무엇을 느꼈는가는「나의 클린트 이스트우드」에 녹아들어 있다고 생각한다.

4

나는 가끔 클린트 이스트우드가「나의 클린트 이스트우드」를 읽으며 피식피식 웃는 걸 상상한다. 클린트 이스트우드는 내게 말할 것이다. "이봐, 친구. 내게 온 걸 환영하네."

해설
Commentary

서부극 연가

정은경 (문학평론가)

오한기의 「나의 클린트 이스트우드」는 클린트 이스트우드에 대한 오마주이자 서부극 연가이다. 주지하다시피 클린트 이스트우드는 마카로니 웨스턴이라 불리는 〈황야의 무법자〉의 그 멋진 건맨이자 일련의 작가주의 영화로 아카데미 상을 수상한 감독이다. 「나의 클린트 이스트우드」는, 주름진 눈에 시가를 잘근잘근 씹으며 권총 한 자루로 무법천지를 평정한 서부극의 '총잡이' 클린트 이스트우드와, 한편 할리우드라는 자본주의 시스템에서 속박당하면서도 '그랜토리노' 같은 고전적 영웅주의 영화를 연출한 집념의 감독, 더불어 공화당원으로 보수적 정의감과 마초적 강인함으로 무장한 채 고집

A Love Song for the Western

Jung Eun-kyoung (literary critic)

Oh Han-ki's "My Clint Eastwood" is a love song for the Western and a homage to Clint Eastwood. As is well known, Clint Eastwood was the proto-typical cool gunman of such macaroni Westerns as *A Fistful of Dollars* and is currently an Oscar-win-ning director of numerous auteur movies. "My Clint Eastwood" presents three versions of Clint East-wood to its readers: the gunman Clint Eastwood of the macaroni Western, gun-toting, cigar-chewing conqueror of the Wild West; The auteur-director Clint Eastwood, director of classical hero movies like *Gran Torino*, engaging in heroic battles against a thoroughly capitalist Hollywood system; And the real-life Clint Eastwood, an aging Republican

스럽게 늙어가고 있는 실제 클린트 이스트우드를 동시에 보여주고 있다. 문제적 인물 '클린트 이스트우드'의 매력은 서부극에서 연출된 '영웅'과 그의 실제 삶의 이력이 겹쳐지고 있는 지점에서 발생한다고 볼 수 있으며, 오한기의 소설 또한 이 지점을 포착하고 있다.

그렇다면 왜 클린트 이스트우드인가? 소설의 주인공은 시나리오 작가 지망생으로 암에 걸려 요양원에 입원한 숙부를 대신하여 펜션과 낚시터를 관리하고 있다. '나'는 고독을 벗삼아 시나리오를 써대지만 공모전에서는 연달아 떨어지고 영화잡지 기자 친구로부터는 '서사가 너무 단순하다' '과거에 붙잡혀 있다'는 등의 비아냥을 듣는다. '찰스 브론슨' '알 파치노'와 같은 '진정한 남자'를 흠모하지만, 실제로 자신은 경원해 마지않는 우디 앨런 같이 "몸은 빼빼 말랐고 눈은 지독히 나빴으며 할 줄 아는 건 수다뿐"인 나약한 남자에 가깝다고 생각한다.

그러던 어느 날 클린트 이스트우드가 펜션을 찾아온다. 고전적 서사에 집착하는 '나'에게 클린트 이스트우드는 약자를 위해 타락한 공권력과 싸우고 악당을 처단한 영웅, 그리고 실제에서도 위대한 감독이자 모범적인 공화당원으로, 총기 소지를 반대하는 감독 마이클 무어

armed with a conservative sense of justice and still exuding a fierce machismo. The problematic figure of Clint Eastwood becomes interesting at the juncture where the Western hero overlaps with the real-life figure. Oh Han-ki's short story captures this character at this very juncture.

But why Clint Eastwood? This story's narrator and protagonist is a would-be screenwriter who manages a guesthouse and a fishing spot for his uncle who has recently been diagnosed with cancer. He continues to write movie pitches in seclusion but his pitches continue to fail in competitions. His former colleague at a movie magazine company criticizes his premises after taking a cursory look at one of them, saying, "the narrative is too simple" and "you're still caught in the past." The narrator adores "true men" like Charles Bronson, Al Pacino, and, of course, Clint Eastwood. Unfortunately, he considers himself to be more in the mold of a Woody Allen, someone he passionately despises because he is "skinny," his "eyesight is extremely bad," and he is "only good at talking."

As it turns out, Clint Eastwood happens to show up at the narrator's guesthouse. To the narrator, Clint Eastwood is a hero, a fierce opponent of corrupt authorities and a champion for the weak, a

따위는 "만약 당신이 우리 집 현관에 카메라를 들고 나타난다면 난 당신을 죽이겠다, 진심이다"라며 한방에 보내버리는 '최고의 남자'이다. 그러나 펜션에 들어선 클린트 이스트우드는 이러한 영웅적 면모와는 무관한 퇴락한 노인일 뿐이다. 카우보이 모자에 낡은 권총을 차고 나타난 이 비현실적인 인물은 구부정한 허리에 온몸에 주름이 가득한 볼품없는 노인, 제작자와 다투고 한국으로 숨어든 도망자, 숙박비가 없어 돈이나 훔치는 좀도둑, 과거의 향수에 젖은 수다쟁이와 허풍쟁이, 젊은 창녀의 몸을 탐하고 여자나 폭행하는 치졸한 인간에 불과했던 것이다.

클린트 이스트우드의 실체에 실망한 주인공은 영화와 현실의 간극을 깨닫는다. 연극이 환상임을 끊임없이 각인시키는 브레히트의 소격효과를 원망하며 "영화가 환상이 아니라면 대체 무엇이란 말인가"라며 한탄해 마지않는 '나'는 영웅 클린트 이스트우드가 아니라 실제 인물이 발 딛고 있는 할리우드라는 강고한 자본주의 시스템, 그리고 그곳에서의 지난한 여정, 그리고 서부극의 종말에 대해 생각한다. 퇴물 총잡이를 형상화한 〈용서받지 못한 자〉로 영웅주의 실체를 고발한 클린트 이

great director and model Republican, and a man who could knock out the likes of the more liberal-minded like Michael Moore. Regarding Michael Moore the narrator remembers Eastwood's words: "Michael, if you ever show up at my house with that camera, I'll shoot you on the spot. I mean it."

However, the Clint Eastwood who appears at his door is a waning old man, totally disconnected from these heroic images. Oh Han-ki's Eastwood shows up wearing a cowboy hat and carrying a broken gun. He is a slight, bent old man, his face full of wrinkles, a runaway who had to sneak into Korea after quarrelling with his producer. He is a petty thief who has to steal to pay his guesthouse fees. A gossip and a gloat wallowing in nostalgia. A crude felon who desperately desires the body of a young prostitute and then assaults her at the slightest provocation.

Disappointed in the true character of Clint Eastwood, this story's protagonist has to confront the gap between cinema and reality. He becomes angry at Brecht and his notion of the "alienation effect," which continues to remind the audience that plays are just illusions. The narrator laments, "What on earth [is] a film if not an illusion?" Instead of finding himself celebrating the hero Clint East-

스트우드는 아카데미감독상과 작품상을 수상했고 이후에도 〈그랜토리노〉 같은 수작을 만들었지만 영화들은 돈벌이가 되지 못했고 퇴물이 되어 쇠락해 가고 잊혀져가고 있을 뿐이다. 이 망가진 영웅의 실체와 영화를 오가며 갈팡질팡하던 주인공은 클린트 이스트우드가 떠나고 숙부가 죽자 펜션을 처분하고 미국 텍사스로 날아간다.

사람들은 서부극의 종말을 이야기하지만, '나'에게 서부극은 여전히 유효한, 아니 '그래야만 한다.' "서부극은 사라지지 않았다. 서부개척시대와 베트남전쟁, 자본주의와 냉전체제, 마르크스와 나치와 무솔리니까지 서부극은 당시 현실과 맥락이 닿아 있고 그 정신은 현재까지 유효했다. 내 생각엔 우리가 오히려 아무 맥락 없이, 혹은 너무나 많은 맥락에 닿아 최면에 걸린 것처럼 비틀거릴 뿐이었다."

'영웅'을 입증할 만한 분명한 선과 악, 직접적인 고통과 화끈한 응징, 그리고 끝없는 사막을 그리워하며 '나'는 비루한 현실에서 벗어나 서부극의 본고장인 텍사스와 리오그란데 강으로 향한 것이다. '올드 텍사스'라는 펍에 한번 들르라는 클린트 이스트우드의 말을 무슨 희

wood, he is forced to consider the strongholds of capitalism and Hollywood, Clint Eastwood's harrowing journey through it, and the end of the Western. While the narrator is aware that Clint Eastwood was an Oscar-winning director for *Unforgiven*, a movie that revealed the truth of Western heroism through the perspective of a retired Old West gunslinger, as well as the director of other critically lauded films like *Gran Torino*, he also realizes his movies have never quite been commercial hits. This Eastwood is outdated, decaying, and forgotten. While wavering between these two poles of thought—the reality of a ruined hero and the world of his movies, the narrator additionally loses his uncle to cancer. He liquidates his share of the guesthouse and flies to Texas.

Although the Western is supposed to be over and done with, to the narrator of this story, the Western is still meaningful. More accurately, the Western *has* to be meaningful:

The Western hadn't died. The Western was closely related to each phase of our reality, from the frontier era through the Vietnam War, from Capitalism and the Cold War system to Marx, Nazism, and Mussolini. The spirit of the Western was

망처럼 가슴에 안고 '진짜 서부극'을 만나기 위해 거리를 헤매지만 펍은 오간 데 없고, 리오그란데 강에는 급류타기를 하러 온 관광객들과 특산품을 팔고 있는 메스티소 인디언이 들끓고 있을 뿐이다. 콘크리트로 메워진 사막, 친절한 현지인, 경찰들의 빈틈없는 치안, 합법적인 매춘, 그리고 온통 호텔과 카지노와 클럽뿐인 시내에서 절망한 주인공은 클린트 이스트우드를 찾아 헤맨다. 결국 '올드 텍사스'가 '블루 씨'라는 클럽으로 바뀌었다는 이야기를 듣고 그곳을 찾아간 주인공은 흑인과 실랑이를 하게 되고, 육탄전을 벌일 찰나 클린트 이스트우드가 나타난다. 흑인의 관자놀이에 총을 겨누고 "이봐, 애송이. 그 손 놓게. 내 친구라네"라며 활짝 웃는 클린트 이스트우드. '어때? 여기가 텍사스야'라는 듯한 그의 표정은 결국 서부극 종말에 대한 완전한 승인을 의미한다. "아름다운 여자로 인해 갈등이 생기고 영웅이 나타나 악인을 처단한다"라는 시나리오는 '블루 씨'라는 막막하고 지저분한 술집에서의 코미디보다 못한 해프닝이 벌어지는 현실로 추락하면서 주인공이 품은 서부극에 대한 환상은 완전히 막을 내리게 되는 것이다.

오한기의 이 단편은 서부극에서 총잡이로 종횡무진

still alive in our contemporary world. It was we who were staggering without any context, or maybe caught within the network of too many contexts as if we had been hypnotized.

The narrator longs for a clear distinction between good and evil and between physical pain and thrilling vengeance. He misses the endless desert of the West, and so the narrator leaves behind his less than ideal reality and heads for Texas and the Rio Grande, home of the Western. As he makes his way West, the narrator especially holds on to the dim hope of Clint Eastwood's invitation for him to drop by the *Old Texas* pub. He wanders the streets of Texas to experience the true West, but the pub is nowhere to be found. Additionally, the Rio Grande is flooded with tourists who come to enjoy rafting and souvenir-selling mestizos. The desert is covered over with concrete, the Texans are polite and amicable, public safety has been thoroughly secured by the police, prostitution has been legalized, and the downtown is populated with nothing but hotels, casinos, and clubs. In total despair, the narrator wanders around increasingly desperately on the lookout for Clint Eastwood.

Eventually, he does find *Old Texas*. Except, at this

했던 클린트 이스트우드, 그리고 영화의 그 총잡이와 다르지 않은 강인한 투지로 할리우드와 미로와 같은 현실에서 고군분투하고 있는, 그러나 패배할 수밖에 없는 클린트 이스트우드에 대한 헌사이자 애도이다. 또한 철저한 자본시스템에 복속된 할리우드와 텍사스라는 우리 시대의 서부극, 우디 앨런의 포스트모더니즘에 대한 절망, 공화당이라는 새로운 악당으로 변한 클린트 이스트우드에 대한 착종된 오마주이기도 하다. 한 가지 덧붙이자면 이 작품은 서부극이라는 낭만적 서사에 대한 그리움을 내세우고 있지만, 한편에서는 이에 대한 체념과 자조적인 조롱을 함께 품고 있다. 그리고 이것은 더 이상 화끈한 드라마를 만들어내지 못하는 문학과 현실에 대한 비가이기도 하다.

'인종 갈등과 베트남전처럼' 더 이상 명확한 적의 실체가 보이지 않는 이 교묘한 현실에서 작가라는 건맨은 어디에다 멋지게 한바탕 총을 쏘아댈 수 있단 말인가. 오한기의 이 슬픈 농담은 정의를 찾아 헤매는 현실의 투사들에게, 그리고 멋진 이야기를 찾아 방황하는 작가들에게 오래 공명하리라.

point it has been reincarnated as *Blue Sea*, and the narrator, perhaps now at his lowest point, scuffles with a man before Clint Eastwood finally appears. Eastwood points a gun at the man's temple and says, "Hey, kid! Let's just relax here! He's my friend." Clint Eastwood smiles at the end, as if to say, "How about that! This is the *real* Texas," finally acknowledging the end of the Western. The classic hero scenario where "a conflict breaking out over a beautiful woman, a hero suddenly appearing to punish the villain" falls apart, turning into nothing more than a scuffle in a dingy nightclub. It ends up more as a sort of a comedy. The narrator's illusions about the Western are finally finished.

Oh's story is ultimately a tribute to both the real-life Clint Eastwood and the remarkable gunman of the Western, now no longer struggling against Western outlaws but engaged in intense, losing battles against a maze-like Hollywood reality. Oh's story is also a complex homage to the Western of our age—the Hollywood and Texas thoroughly subjugated by all-consuming capitalist systems—, the despair over a post-modern reality represented by Woody Allen, and a Clint Eastwood turned villain and Republican. Additionally, although this story seems to yearn for the Western romantic

정은경 문학평론가. 1969년 서울에서 태어나고 고려대 독문과와 국문과 대학원을 졸업했다. 2003년 《세계일보》에 평론 「웃음과 망각의 수사학」으로 등단하였으며, 현재 비평 전문 반년간 지 《작가와비평》과 아시아 문학전문 바이링궐 계간지 《아시아》의 편집위원으로 활동하고 있다. 2005년 고려대학교에서 「한국 근대소설에 나타난 악의 표상」으로 문학박사학위를 취득했으며, 현재 원광대 교수로 재직 중이다. 저서로 『디아스포라 문학』 『한국 근대소설에 나타난 惡의 표상 연구』 『지도의 암실』 등이 있다.

narrative, it is also a self-mockery of the Western-lover's yearning for these bygone stories as well as a resignation to the reality of this loss. It is an elegy to literature and a reality that no longer seems capable of generating drama of this kind anymore.

In a shrewd contemporary reality where clear enemies like "racial conflicts or the Vietnam War" no longer exist, where can the writer aim his weapons and carry out that final, classic showdown? This tragic-comic tale by Oh will resonate for years to come, appealing to fighters searching for justice, and writers in search of truly captivating drama.

Jung Eun-kyoung Born in Seoul in 1969, Jung Eun-kyoung graduated from korea university after majoring in German and korean literature. She made her literary debut by winning ***the Segye Ilbo*** Spring Literary competition in criticism with the article "A Rhetoric of Laughter and Forgetting: on Song Sok-ze." Her published works include ***Literature of Diaspora, A Study of the Representation of Evil in Modern Korean Novels***, and A Darkroom of Map. She is currently a professor at the Division of korean Language and Literature at Wonkwang University and a member of the editorial board of the literary journal ***Writer and Criticism*** as well as the magazine of Asian literature ***ASIA***.

비평의 목소리
Critical Acclaim

이야기에 이야기를 주렁주렁 매달리게 하는 내러티브의 풍성한 구성력이 이 소설의 일차적 미덕이라면, 인간과 삶에 대한 이해를 풍부하게 해줄 다채로운 문화적 경험을 통해 한국소설이 넘지 못하는 경계를 과감하게 떨치고 이야기로서의 보편성을 마련하는 지점에서 이 소설만의 독특성이 확보된다. 함께 응모한 「더 웬즈데이」도 당선작으로 손색이 없는 작품이었다. 「파라솔이 접힌 오후」를 당선작으로 선정한 것이라기보다 오한기 씨를 당선자로 선정했다는 표현이 더 적절할 것이다. (……) 한국문학의 쇄신을 이끌어줄 문단의 차기 주자로 기대해도 좋을 오한기 씨를 당선자로 선정하는 데

The primary virtue of this short story might be its rich organizational skill, allowing it to cluster various stories together. Its most singular virtue, however, is its universal quality: it dares to cross Korean fiction's conventional boundaries by incorporating various cultural experiences that expand our understanding of human beings and their lives. "The Wednesday," another piece that Oh submitted together with this work, is also worthy of publishing. It would be more accurate to say that we selected the writer Oh Han-ki rather than his story, "Afternoon of a Folded Parasol."... We judges all agreed to recommend that Oh be selected as one of leaders of the next generation authors who would re-

이견은 없었다.

소영현, 백가흠, 「2012 신인추천작 심사평」,

《현대문학》 NO. 690, 현대문학, 2012.

new Korean literature.

So Yeong-hyeon, Paik Ga-huim, "Judges' Remarks on Recommending a 2012 Debut Author's Work," *Hyundae Munhak* 690 (2012)

K-픽션 004
나의 클린트 이스트우드

2014년 8월 29일 초판 1쇄 인쇄 | 2014년 9월 5일 초판 1쇄 발행

지은이 오한기 | **옮긴이** 전승희 | **펴낸이** 김재범
기획위원 정은경, 전성태, 이경재
편집 정수인, 이은혜, 윤단비, 김형욱 | **관리** 박신영 | **디자인** 이춘희
펴낸곳 (주)아시아 | **출판등록** 2006년 1월 27일 제406-2006-000004호
주소 서울특별시 동작구 서달로 161-1(흑석동 100-16)
전화 02.821.5055 | **팩스** 02.821.5057 | **홈페이지** www.bookasia.org
ISBN 979-11-5662-043-3(set) | 979-11-5662-047-1(04810)
값은 뒤표지에 있습니다.

K-Fiction 004
My Clint Eastwood

Written by Oh Han-ki | **Translated by** Jeon Seung-hee
Published by Asia Publishers | 161-1, Seodal-ro, Dongjak-gu, Seoul, Korea
Homepage Address www.bookasia.org | **Tel**. (822).821.5055 | **Fax**. (822).821.5057
First published in Korea by Asia Publishers 2014
ISBN 979-11-5662-043-3(set) | 979-11-5662-047-1(04810)

바이링궐 에디션 한국 대표 소설

한국문학의 가장 중요하고 첨예한 문제의식을 가진 작가들의 대표작을 주제별로 선정!
하버드 한국학 연구원 및 세계 각국의 한국문학 전문 번역진이 참여한 번역 시리즈!
미국 하버드대학교와 컬럼비아대학교 동아시아학과, 캐나다 브리티시컬럼비아대학교 아시아학과 등 해외 대학에서 교재로 채택!

바이링궐 에디션 한국 대표 소설 set 1

분단 Division

01 병신과 머저리-**이청준** The Wounded-**Yi Cheong-jun**
02 어둠의 혼-**김원일** Soul of Darkness-**Kim Won-il**
03 순이삼촌-**현기영** Sun-i Samch'on-**Hyun Ki-young**
04 엄마의 말뚝 1-**박완서** Mother's Stake I-**Park Wan-suh**
05 유형의 땅-**조정래** The Land of the Banished-**Jo Jung-rae**

산업화 Industrialization

06 무진기행-**김승옥** Record of a Journey to Mujin-**Kim Seung-ok**
07 삼포 가는 길-**황석영** The Road to Sampo-**Hwang Sok-yong**
08 아홉 켤레의 구두로 남은 사내-**윤흥길** The Man Who Was Left as Nine Pairs of Shoes-**Yun Heung-gil**
09 돌아온 우리의 친구-**신상웅** Our Friend's Homecoming-**Shin Sang-ung**
10 원미동 시인-**양귀자** The Poet of Wŏnmi-dong-**Yang Kwi-ja**

여성 Women

11 중국인 거리-**오정희** Chinatown-**Oh Jung-hee**
12 풍금이 있던 자리-**신경숙** The Place Where the Harmonium Was-**Shin Kyung-sook**
13 하나코는 없다-**최윤** The Last of Hanak'o-**Ch'oe Yun**
14 인간에 대한 예의-**공지영** Human Decency-**Gong Ji-young**
15 빈처-**은희경** Poor Man's Wife-**Eun Hee-kyung**

바이링궐 에디션 한국 대표 소설 set 2

자유 Liberty

16 필론의 돼지-**이문열** Pilon's Pig-**Yi Mun-yol**
17 슬로우 불릿-**이대환** Slow Bullet-**Lee Dae-hwan**
18 직선과 독가스-**임철우** Straight Lines and Poison Gas-**Lim Chul-woo**
19 깃발-**홍희담** The Flag-**Hong Hee-dam**
20 새벽 출정-**방현석** Off to Battle at Dawn-**Bang Hyeon-seok**

사랑과 연애 Love and Love Affairs

21 별을 사랑하는 마음으로-**윤후명** With the Love for the Stars-**Yun Hu-myong**
22 목련공원-**이승우** Magnolia Park-**Lee Seung-u**
23 칼에 찔린 자국-**김인숙** Stab-**Kim In-suk**
24 회복하는 인간-**한강** Convalescence-**Han Kang**
25 트렁크-**정이현** In the Trunk-**Jeong Yi-hyun**

남과 북 South and North

26 판문점-**이호철** Panmunjom-**Yi Ho-chol**
27 수난 이대-**하근찬** The Suffering of Two Generations-**Ha Geun-chan**
28 분지-**남정현** Land of Excrement-**Nam Jung-hyun**
29 봄 실상사-**정도상** Spring at Silsangsa Temple-**Jeong Do-sang**
30 은행나무 사랑-**김하기** Gingko Love-**Kim Ha-kee**

바이링궐 에디션 한국 대표 소설 set 3

서울 Seoul

31 눈사람 속의 검은 항아리-**김소진** The Dark Jar within the Snowman-**Kim So-jin**
32 오후, 가로지르다-**하성란** Traversing Afternoon-**Ha Seong-nan**
33 나는 봉천동에 산다-**조경란** I Live in Bongcheon-dong-**Jo Kyung-ran**
34 그렇습니까? 기린입니다-**박민규** Is That So? I'm A Giraffe-**Park Min-gyu**
35 성탄특선-**김애란** Christmas Specials-**Kim Ae-ran**

전통 Tradition

36 무자년의 가을 사흘-**서정인** Three Days of Autumn, 1948-**Su Jung-in**
37 유자소전-**이문구** A Brief Biography of Yuja-**Yi Mun-gu**
38 향기로운 우물 이야기-**박범신** The Fragrant Well-**Park Bum-shin**
39 월행-**송기원** A Journey under the Moonlight-**Song Ki-won**
40 협죽도 그늘 아래-**성석제** In the Shade of the Oleander-**Song Sok-ze**

아방가르드 Avant-garde

41 아겔다마-**박상륭** Akeldama-**Park Sang-ryoong**
42 내 영혼의 우물-**최인석** A Well in My Soul-**Choi In-seok**
43 당신에 대해서-**이인성** On You-**Yi In-seong**
44 회색 時-**배수아** Time In Gray-**Bae Su-ah**
45 브라운 부인-**정영문** Mrs. Brown-**Jung Young-moon**

바이링궐 에디션 한국 대표 소설 set 4

디아스포라 Diaspora

46 속옷-**김남일** Underwear-**Kim Nam-il**
47 상하이에 두고 온 사람들-**공선옥** People I Left in Shanghai-**Gong Sun-ok**
48 모두에게 복된 새해-**김연수** Happy New Year to Everyone-**Kim Yeon-su**
49 코끼리-**김재영** The Elephant-**Kim Jae-young**
50 먼지별-**이경** Dust Star-**Lee Kyung**

가족 Family

51 혜자의 눈꽃-**천승세** Hye-ja's Snow-Flowers-**Chun Seung-sei**
52 아베의 가족-**전상국** Ahbe's Family-**Jeon Sang-guk**
53 문 앞에서-**이동하** Outside the Door-**Lee Dong-ha**
54 그리고, 축제-**이혜경** And Then the Festival-**Lee Hye-kyung**
55 봄밤-**권여선** Spring Night-**Kwon Yeo-sun**

유머 Humor

56 오늘의 운세-**한창훈** Today's Fortune-**Han Chang-hoon**
57 새-**전성태** Bird-**Jeon Sung-tae**
58 밀수록 다시 가까워지는-**이기호** So Far, and Yet So Near-**Lee Ki-ho**
59 유리방패-**김중혁** The Glass Shield-**Kim Jung-hyuk**
60 전당포를 찾아서-**김종광** The Pawnshop Chase-**Kim Chong-kwang**

바이링궐 에디션 한국 대표 소설 set 5

관계 Relationship

61 도둑견습 - **김주영** Robbery Training-**Kim Joo-young**
62 사랑하라, 희망 없이 - **윤영수** Love, Hopelessly-**Yun Young-su**
63 봄날 오후, 과부 셋 - **정지아** Spring Afternoon, Three Widows-**Jeong Ji-a**
64 유턴 지점에 보물지도를 묻다 - **윤성희** Burying a Treasure Map at the U-turn-**Yoon Sung-hee**
65 쁘이거나 쯔이거나 - **백가흠** Puy, Thuy, Whatever-**Paik Ga-huim**

일상의 발견 Discovering Everyday Life

66 나는 음식이다 - **오수연** I Am Food-**Oh Soo-yeon**
67 트럭 - **강영숙** Truck-**Kang Young-sook**
68 통조림 공장 - **편혜영** The Canning Factory-**Pyun Hye-young**
69 꽃 - **부희령** Flowers-**Pu Hee-ryoung**
70 피의일요일 - **윤이형** BloodySunday-**Yun I-hyeong**

금기와 욕망 Taboo and Desire